Dear Mom,

I'm sorry

Book 1

In the Family Journals

Dear Mom, I'm sorry

By

Mary O'Hora

This book is for you.

No matter what debates it encourages or uncomfortable conversations it might prompt. It's so that the next time you need to tell someone you need a mental health moment, they'll have some idea of what you mean.

Communicate, keep the conversation going. The end is never the answer.

Warning: Although fictional, this is an end-of-life journal and therefore touches on a variety of topics which some readers may find distressing.

Epilogue

Dear Mom,

I grabbed this notebook to write you a last goodbye. I hope you can hear me when I say I love you more than anything, and I pray that one day you'll be able to understand why I'm doing this. Why I no longer have a choice, I simply can't continue.

There is not a doubt in my mind that you will struggle to accept this for the rest of your life. That your 'logical' mind will demand reasons. Opening a blank page, I started a list. I wasn't even halfway through when I accepted that for each and every reason I've written, you would need a detailed explanation. Even with my growing list, there will never be enough paper or time to demonstrate it all to you in such detail. To make you feel how I do.

1

Dear Mom, I'm sorry

The truth is, I no longer want to be here, but I need you to promise not to blame yourself. I may not fully comprehend what happiness feels like, but I know hopelessness and despair to the core of my bones. They are my daily companions. I don't want them to become yours too.

Out of all the things in the world I am 100% certain of, your love for me is one of them. You have loved me since the day I was born, and only ever wanted the best for me. Unfortunately, you can't possibly understand what it's like to live in my body and to be stuck with these broken feelings. I am certain that once you realize how difficult it is for me, you'll find a way to let me go. You will grant me your blessing, and I will never need to wake up to another day of suffering.

So, that's what I intend to do. Write in this journal until I trust you can appreciate how hard life is for me. Sharing my despair and fears with you until I am convinced you won't want to read anymore. Unveiling my lies until you are finally ready to say goodbye.

If you're reading this, I'm already gone. Maybe it's just days since or perhaps it's weeks, but I trust, eventually you will come to terms with reality, that this was my choice. If I could have done things differently, I would have. I hope that this truth, no matter how tough it is to read, will set you free.

I love you, Mom.

Chelsie

X O X

Dear Mom, I'm sorry

Chapter 1

For 3 days, I've debated how much detail I'm willing to expose. It's hard. There are so many things that you think you know, but you don't. I'm worried that you will feel as if it's all been a lie, like I've been masquerading my entire life.

Our lives are filled with misconceptions. Most of the time, I go along with whatever's easiest, so no one needs to worry about me. I choose the path that will shine the dimmest light.

Remember when Hannah and I were little at the carnival? I was about 6 and Hannah would have been 9. We were fishing for ducks. You know, the game where everyone wins a prize? Hannah hooked her duck first. She jumped up and down excitedly. The vendor removed the bright yellow duck from her hook and reached behind her for a wicker basket, which she placed on the ledge in front of us. "You can choose any prize from here, ok honey?" The lady picked up the basket and offered it closer, but Hannah's face crumpled. She had been hoping for one of the stuffed animals displayed on the back wall of the booth. Reluctantly, she picked out a set of bangles.

After much practice, I eventually caught a duck too. I had several near misses. With each attempt, I thought it was hooked, lifting my empty rod as the little duck continued floating in the makeshift pond. Hannah kept pointing out other ducks for me to try to hook, but I really wanted this exact one. A small bit of his eye was scratched off and his hook was bent. I was certain nobody else ever chose him. I was determined to catch him. "Oh, we have a winner." The lady exclaimed loudly for people passing by to hear. As she lifted my rod, I noticed the little duck had a gold star on his underbelly. "Choose any item from the back wall, young lady." She waved her wrinkled hand towards the large stuffed animals, and I assessed all the prizes I might potentially choose.

There was a rainbow-colored llama, a wolf with pointy ears, a frizzy-haired troll and even a purple penguin. I looked from one to the next and felt nothing. Absolutely nothing. The woman smiled at me kindly. Hannah was bouncing from one foot to the other, eagerly pointing at the frizzy-haired troll. I tried hard to *feel* something. Excitement to have won. Anticipation of my prize even, but it was pointless. I pointed towards the troll. The lady reached behind the stall and used a long pole to unhook the toy. She passed me the ugly blue-eyed doll with the wild pink hair. "What will you name her?" she asked? I shrugged my shoulders and stared back at her, not knowing what to say. "Here we are now folks, another big winner!" Her voice echoed over to the other families nearby, encouraging them to come and test their luck. I mumbled my thanks and held the plush toy close, urging it to help me *feel*.

I was aware of Hannah looking enviously at my prize, and on impulse, I offered it to her. Her eyes danced with delight as she held it in her arms. She took my arm and passed it through the bracelets. The thin metal scratched the skin on my hand as she forced them around my small but chubby fingers. "I'm kind of too grown up for these bracelets, Chelsie, but look, they're perfect for you." She smiled as she released my arm and the cool steel circles fell against my wrist. I looked at them, glistening in the sun. Hoping the sight of them on my arm might bring me the same excitement and joy as the troll had brought her, but I was empty.

Hannah leaned in and hugged me tightly. "You're the best little sister anyone could ever have." She informed me. I still felt nothing. However, in that moment, I realized my actions had given Hannah the feelings I would never have. Her bright smile beamed at me. I had made her happy. She pulled me along by the hand as we rushed back to the bench where you and dad were sitting with baby Ben. She showed you her prize proudly, and you took turns making crazy hairstyles on her ugly doll.

You said you loved my pretty bracelets, and I smiled back, so you would think that I loved them too. If I didn't, you would have asked me questions. What was wrong? Didn't I love my new bangles? Did I want the troll doll back? Was I jealous of Hannah? If I didn't smile and play along, questions ensued. It was easier to fake a smile and pretend to have feelings, just like everyone else.

Mom, that was my very first memory of when I realized that even though I can't experience emotions, I can help others. I can give them my good feelings, so at least someone gets to have them, even if it's not me. At least if I pass them on, they're not wasted. It is also the first time I learned it was simpler to pretend than to be honest.

From that day onwards, I still tried to understand feelings. I studied Hannah when she was excited and even tried to practice her moves. Smile, clap hands, high five and jump up and down. I learned to mirror her moods perfectly, but the feelings never came. The more I pretended, the emptier I became, but I noticed other people, those surrounding me, were happier when I acted happy, too. So, I learned to watch for cues and to play my part. When I smiled and bounced in place, you would nudge Dad. The two of you smiling at each other, then at Hannah and me. My smiles allowed you to be happy. They permitted you to relax.

Dear Mom, I'm sorry

Chapter 2

School. The best and worst part of my day. The best because I don't need to act so intently. No one cares how I feel or how I'm doing, so I don't need to waste a lot of effort *pretending*. Some days I'm exhausted from the pretense of being ok. The 6-hour reprieve gives me a break from trying to remember the appropriate responses. I can fade into the background there, and remain unremarkable.

The teachers like me because I'm quiet. My homework is always complete, I achieve good grades and never interrupt. Preferring to spend time in my bedroom doing my homework means I'm usually ahead of the class curriculum.

Time out of the classroom is something I dread. 5-minute changes between each class, lunch and outdoor walks are my worse times of the day. The other kids have too much energy and I loiter in the hallways, hoping to be left alone. Eyes down in a book or pretending to search in my school bag so as not to draw any unwanted attention to myself. Kids are opportunists. They pick on the easiest, closest target. Observing their mean behavior over the years has allowed me to learn the necessary techniques to stay out of their way and let their inevitable teasing fall on another student instead. Occasionally, I put myself in the line of fire if I sense the other kid can't take it. I kind of step in to give them the day off, so to speak. They think the bullies have just chosen to pick on me today. They don't realize that I purposely engineered to take their crap for the day to give them a break. None of it matters anyway.

The bullies can't face their own insecurities. I've been watching them for years. Stepping on the rest of us to make themselves feel better. Me and the other targets are just pawns in their games.

No one cares about us. When I say no one, I don't mean you; I mean the other kids, the staff, the rest of the world. You might think it could be different. If only I had told you the truth, but I've watched other kids tell and trust me, it only intensifies the bullying. It never resolves it.

Unfortunately, it's a case of he who shouts loudest, wins. There's a boy in my math class called Max. He's quiet, with large framed glasses and the tightest curls you could imagine. In the first few weeks of school, he sat at the popular kids' lunch table and would laugh and joke with everyone. There were rumors that Bethany Wilkinson had a crush on him. However, Jordan Pearson in grade 10 also liked Bethany and did not welcome the competition that Max brought. By the second week of school, Jordan had started a rumor that Max had the smallest dick in school. Whether it might be true or not was irrelevant. The gossip spread throughout the school like wildfire. There was even a meme about him posted on the schools 'losers of St. Michaels' Facebook page, (yes there really is a page). Max was instantly exiled from the popular kids' lunch table and now walks around the track field during lunch time, avoiding the rest of us, as much as he can.

Parents think they can help, demanding a meeting with the principal, but they're so wrong. After Max's Mom complained to the school, he became known as the 'wee wiener boy'. Kids would ask him where his mommy was every time they crossed him in the hallways. Her visit only added to the taunting and teasing.

I've been watching Jordan Pearson since kindergarten. He has been a bully since his first day at elementary school. His mom and dad are drug addicts and he's often placed in temporary foster homes where he is ignored if lucky, and abused if not. In grade 7, he moved in with his grandma and it was the first year he ever made a friend at school. He stopped fighting other kids. It appeared like he was finally getting the chance to just be a kid.

Later that year, his grandma died, and he was placed with another foster family. Shortly after, he came to school with deep purple bruises on his arm. No one else noticed. He wore ¾ sleeve baseball shirts to try to hide them. The one advantage to watching people your entire life is that you get a kind of sixth sense about them. I understand body language without even trying. I notice small details that hold bigger meanings. I'm hyper-aware of my environment from all the years of studying and learning.

During lunch, I found Jordan at an empty table. I asked him if he was ok. "You should see the other guy." He tried to laugh it off, but his eyes looked sad. The dark circles underneath them seemed deeper than usual, as though his eyeballs had further sunken into his skull.

"I'm sorry to hear about your grandma." I spoke quietly to ensure none of the other students at the nearby picnic table could hear me.

He shook his head and shrugged. "You're born, you die. It's the cycle of life." His voice cracked ever so slightly and instinctively I reached out my hand and placed it on his arm. He flinched as a spark of fear filled his eyes. "Don't ever touch me again freak." He yelled in my face and that's when I realized Jordan's chance was gone now. He has needed to keep his guard up his whole life and with his grandma gone, he would need to continue with the false bravado.

The school, his family, nor even society are going to help him. He's just another statistic. The cycle never ends. In September, there will be another Max and the whole messed-up cycle will repeat itself. It will never change, and there will always be people who just aren't as tough as others.

High school is a trauma for so many kids. One girl has been jumped 6 times so far this year and guess what's happened about that? Nothing. That's right because the girl who keeps jumping her is the star rugby player and apparently our school cares more about trophies than they do about their students' well-being. She was suspended for 2 days, but when she returned, she was more popular than before. The whole system is broken, including the kids.

The walk home is my favorite part of the day. I take a really long time to gather my things and tidy my locker at the end of class. I never leave the building until I'm sure that most of the other *walkers* are at least halfway home.

The crisp air hits my face. I button up my denim jacket and head towards the trail. It's been raining all weekend, and the ground is swampy. I kick up the damp leaves underfoot, navigating the path from the shortcut between school and our subdivision. As I exit the clearing, the closest thing I know to happiness brings a smile to my face. At the end of the street, I see my only friend waiting for me. He runs up and down the chain-link fence, excited to greet me. I lengthen my stride, eager to visit with him before he gets called back inside.

As I reach the corner of the yard, the sandy, blonde mutt wags his tail vigorously. Sitting by the edge of the property, under the large oak tree, I search in my bag for the leftover ham roll I saved for Luke. I don't actually know Luke's real name, but he seems like a Luke to me, so that's what I call him. Unwrapping the roll, I pull off small bites and feed them to him through the fence. He slobbers all over my fingers and eats the leftovers hungrily. I don't think his owner feeds him very much. I've only caught brief glimpses of the old man when he's come hobbling to the green front door, yelling for Luke to get inside. He never calls for him by name but refers to him as, boy, with a plethora of swear words attached. He appears in the doorway just as I feed my friend the last morsel of lunch. He steadies himself by holding onto the frame of the house, whistling for the dog to come inside. Maybe he's a drinker? Perhaps he forgets to feed Luke, and that's why he's always hungry? The dog makes his way reluctantly back to the house, his fluffy tail no longer wagging, but hanging limp between his legs. Glancing back towards the hedges in my direction forlornly. In that instant, I can truly understand how Luke feels. He's my only friend, as I am his. The green door closes. I gather my bag and leave my sheltered spot, hoping the grumpy old man didn't notice me lurking by the bushes.

I try to erase the image of Luke looking back at me with his big sad eyes and prepare to jump back into character. The *Chelsie* you all love to see coming home. The one I pretend to be when I'm not alone.

Pushing open the front door, the smell of roast chicken fills my nostrils. The warm air engulfs me, welcoming me home from the cool air outside. I hang up my coat, put away my shoes and come to join you in the kitchen.

"Chelsie, you're home! How was your day?" You ask as soon as I enter the room. Worry lines crease your smooth forehead, but your voice is filled with hope. I no longer fill you in on the real events of my schooldays, as I couldn't take watching your face crumple with sadness anymore. Now, I pretend everything is great and often fill you in on what we learned that day to distract you from delving deeper.

"How was Anna? Did you have lunch together?" You enquire about Anna almost daily. I mentioned her once months ago, and from that one casual sentence, you deduced that she and I were best friends. The first few times you enquired about her, I answered as if it was indeed the case and it made your smile so wide that I didn't want to correct you. You seemed almost relieved that I had finally found a friend. In fact, she left our school 2 months ago because of the extensive bullying she was subjected to, but every day I answer your questions about her and pretend she's still around. It's completely ridiculous but I have no idea how to stop the pretense now.

This is my first admission to you about the lies I tell you daily, but it won't be the last and I really need you to understand that it's not your fault. It's me. I don't know how to react or behave correctly. I'm constantly guessing what I think people want me to say or do, only to find I'm stuck in the patterns and lies I've woven. The lies make everyone more comfortable. That time I mistakenly mentioned Anna, you announced to the dinner table that I had a new friend and how wonderful it was. You even encouraged dad to ask me questions about her when he phoned for his nightly check-in. How could I now admit that I barely knew the girl? It was so much easier to just go along with it. I've invented a whole persona, so I can keep you updated on her. I'm embarrassed that it's simply one more false reality in my world.

Dear Mom, I'm sorry

Chapter 3

Today is wear pink to school day, raising awareness of the school's latest anti-bullying campaign. These fake lip service days are like torture to me. Last year I feigned a bad stomach, so you let me stay home. If I dodged it again this year, your mom's intuition would kick in and you would sense something was wrong. Your concern would lead to more questions so, reluctantly I make my way to school.

During assembly, a spokesperson from each class gives a short speech about what bullying means to them and how we must all stick together. The irony is that 90% of the kids making these speeches are the actual bullies of the school. Their parents are on the PTA. They're the head cheerleader, or dating the football star. They have a false popularity, which prevents anyone from standing up to them.

Teachers, parents and other kids are afraid to call them out in case the negative attention ends up on them. It's a vicious circle.

Maddy Talbot is our school's most popular girl. Her social media posts are all anti-bullying and mental health matters. She is single-handedly responsible for 2 girls leaving our school this year. Her mocking, mean girl personality is downplayed as teasing and joking by teachers. The meaner she becomes, the more popular she is. Kids are afraid to stand up to her and choose to support her appalling behavior rather than face the risk of being subjected to her mean girl antics.

Last September, during suicide awareness week, she showed up at school with a yellow ribbon tattoo on her forearm. At lunchtime, she distributed ribbon-shaped cookies to the most popular tables in the cafeteria, and the recipients applauded and cheered her. During the end-of-week assembly, Mr. Garner said he and the staff wished to express their thanks to Maddy for all her hard work. I sat there dumbfounded. Am I sleeping? Is this a nightmare? How are all these smart, educated people being taken in so easily with a few cookies and fake smiles?

Fast forward to mid-October, when Amber Strauss was in hospital after a failed suicide attempt. She could no longer take the constant harassment she endured daily from Maddy. No one called Maddy out, no one stood up to her or forced her to face the consequences of her actions. She arranged lunchtime awareness rallies with bright, colorful signs. Her hand-painted posters decorated every hall and classroom in the school. People forgot about Amber or how she was coping. She never returned to our school and from the small glimpses I've seen on her social media, she seems to be thriving now that she's away from such a toxic environment.

Almost a year later and nothing has changed. Maddy is still a self-appointed spokesperson for mental health at our school and remains the biggest social media bully in our town.

I accept you'll be surprised to discover this. You've been friends with Jane Talbot since your own high school days. You and Jane have encouraged a friendship between Maddy and me since we were toddlers. Even as babies, Maddy would snatch anything I had first. For years, I would give in and play whatever games she wanted even when she bent and twisted the rules to suit herself. It was easier to give in than to explain why I didn't want to be her friend, why I didn't want to go to her house for playdates whilst you and Jane sipped cappuccinos on their back deck. But again, the lies kept piling and by high school, you genuinely thought Maddy and I were friends.

I don't think I have ever voiced out loud that I no longer experience emotions and live simply with a constant numbness where my sadness used to be. I kind of just assumed it's a fact we've all accepted. It is what it is. For most of my years growing up, I simply copied those around me, sometimes girls at school, but mainly Hannah. In the 6th grade, we had a nurse visit us weekly for sex education. I wasn't particularly interested in the anatomy part, but I was enthralled with the emotional aspect of growing up. Did you know that during puberty, hormones increase in our body, our emotions and moods change?

"Fluctuations in your sex hormones, estrogen, progesterone, and testosterone can often seem like a roller coaster of emotions in your teen years." Nurse Jenny informed us. She spoke of overwhelming feelings and I drank in every word. I would soon be normal, like everyone else. I wouldn't need to gauge those around me and play a part. My hormones were going to kick in any day and bring with them a whirlwind of emotion. Granted, some of those feelings might be negative, but I was positive I could manage them when they arrived.

Later that year, I started my period, months passed and acne joined me on my hormonal journey, but the emotions never came. Physically, my body reacted in all the right ways to puberty, but emotionally I was still numb. By Grade 8, nurse Jenny had covered everything we might ever want to know. She taught us the difference between anxiety and depression. Bullying and manipulation. The dangers and risks of alcohol and drugs. There wasn't a subject that she would not talk to us about. Nothing was taboo. She regularly encouraged us at the end of the class to spend time in the evening googling questions we may have and to bring back the info to share with the rest of the class. "Girls, if you have found yoga helpful to cope with keeping a sense of calm, share that info with your girlfriends, encourage them to try it as well. Boys, if an hour lifting weights or running after school helps release some of that pent-up testosterone, then recognize when your body needs that extra outlet. Practicing self-care is paramount during adolescence. You need to look after yourselves. Remember, your emotions or reactions to certain situations may not be your fault, but they are your responsibility. You need to find the right ways to cope and heal throughout your life. Starting those healthy practices now while you're young is great for your future mental health." Nurse Jenny was a great advocate for sharing our experiences to bring us closer and to understand each other better and although I didn't relate to the other students, I spent most of my evenings visiting the websites she recommended.

I stumbled upon support groups and forums where there were people just like me. At first, I was absolutely obsessed, reading new posts and people's advice every spare second I could. I wanted to learn everything there was to know. I was like a sponge, soaking up new knowledge daily. The more I learned, the higher chance I had of becoming better, of being normal.

It was then that I learned about emotional blunting. Finally, I had a diagnosis I understood. Unfortunately, it also seemed like a dead end to my own journey. Online, there were other kids like me, emotionless, but there were also 40 and

50-year-old adults. Nothing ever changed for them. They're still posting on message boards. Trying to understand themselves or make a connection with another. They still haven't made sense of their lives. Still acting and pretending to others around them. Or worse, they've voluntarily isolated themselves from those who love them. Anything to end the constant acting, every minute of every hour of every day

It was the first time I ever admitted to myself that I didn't want to play any role for the rest of my life.

Dear Mom, I'm sorry

Chapter 4

This morning you woke me, sitting on the edge of my bed. "Hey there sleepy head, how did you sleep?" I grunt and roll back into my duvet. I'm unsure what time it is, but it feels early, too early for a chat. "It's beautiful out." You announce, pulling back the blackout curtains and sliding open the window. A stream of light blinds my sleepy eyes.

A small, silent sigh escapes my lips. I sit up, rubbing my eyelids to clear their blurry vision. You bend to collect my slipper socks off the floor and drop them into the white linen laundry basket. Continuing the room inspection, you rearrange little trinkets on the shelf above my desk. Fully alert now, I tilt my head to one side and raise my eyebrows. Not especially keen to find out what this intrusion is all about, but aware that you won't be leaving until you have said your piece.

"Chelsie is everything ok at school?" You ask. Your voice sounds hesitant, cautious even. I know you're asking to reassure yourself all is well and so I nod casually from my bed.

"Sure. Why what's up?" Stretching my arms, I yawn exaggeratively, hoping you might take the hint and leave. Another hour or two of sleep is definitely required.

You hand me a few sheets of paper, which I recognize as the sign-up sheets for next year's school trip to Europe. "I saw these poking out of your bag and I'm wondering why you haven't asked me to fill them in?" A shadow crosses your face. I shake my head, eager to comfort you.

I leaf through the sheets, biding my time to concoct a believable excuse. What would it be like to tell you everything? The whole horrible truth. Allow the words to spill from my mouth and never stop. Confess my intentions. Admit that by the time this trip comes around, I will no longer be here.

All hell would break loose. An emergency appointment with the hospital psychiatrist, Dr. Ingram, would be made. You would call dad in Florida so the two of you could talk in hushed tones. Aunt Regina would appear to invite Ben for a sleepover, allowing you to concentrate on me 100%.

You would delay calling Hannah at University until a solution was found. No need for her to worry unnecessarily. She wouldn't be able to leave the students from her summer job, anyway. You would clasp your hands together after every sentence, as though another problem had been resolved. The skin on your bottom lip, chapped and broken, where you had dug your teeth in too deep. Everything within your power would be done to help 'fix me'. I would watch as a passive participant, but sooner or later your worry and concern would force me to act. Pretend to be better, relieving you from some of the stress. Just for a day or two. But those few days would turn into weeks, months, years, even. We would be back to where we are now. Pretending, lying.

Is a lie really a sin when it protects others, though? I don't want to think my entire life has been a lie. I hope that my acting throughout these years will leave you with enough memories when I'm gone. Memories you can share and reminisce when you're all together.

"Oh, I completely forgot to give you the info about the trip." I shake my head and roll my eyes to signal what

31

an airhead I am. "Thank goodness you've found them and reminded me". I stretch the widest smile across my face, eager to ease your concerns. You laugh and ruffle my hair. Instantly grateful that it was a simple mistake and not a sign of trouble ahead, as you feared.

Chattering away, I embellish the idea of the trip, and your smile grows wider and wider, listening to the false hopes and plans that lay ahead.

You pick up a pen from my wooden desk and begin filling in the forms. Your eyes widen and dance excitedly as you read out details of planned excursions and stopovers. Unable to locate your check book, you search the entire house. I want to tell you it doesn't matter and not to waste your time looking for it, but after forty-five minutes you screech victoriously, "found it!"

Watching you fill out the cheque, so proudly for a trip I would never take, is a memory I hope to forget. Knowing that you will need to request a refund of the deposit later. How I wish there was another alternative to save you from further hurt.

Why can't there be a solution that would end my hurt without starting yours? I used to think that I could continue playing the role of pretending until you passed away. Then I could end my life guilt-free. The flaw in my plan is sometimes I wonder if I can make it another minute, another day, so how would I hold on for years? Even through a broken heart, you will still have hope for happiness. My absence will bring you tears and sadness, but you will still have Hannah and Ben. Drinks by the pool at Aunt Regina's will welcome you on a hot summer's day. Daffodils will remain your favorite flowers. Air will continue to fill your lungs, and feelings will flood your heart. I don't doubt how desolate life might seem, but only for a short while. The pain will subside, your mind eventually accepting my choice. Your life will continue, but mine would never even start. I would just exist and it's not enough. It's too hard.

Dear Mom, I'm sorry

Chapter 5

With the turn of every page, you will try to figure out where you should have helped me more. Your catalog of *what ifs* and *if onlys* will be full. You can't help someone feel though, Mom, not when they're incomplete.

That's how I think of myself. Everyone else is living and experiencing, except me. I'm already dead in this vibrant world. Last year, I wrote down all the things that might help me feel; it was a long list, I would add to it regularly, but the primary emotions were suffering, excitement, fear and happiness. I didn't omit sadness, but I remember vividly the days before my diagnosis and medication. Nothing will ever erase the torment or grief I had lived with every day. I will never go back to that. It wasn't a life. Revisiting those dark times is not an option.

I mean is this a fair choice? No sensation or live in the darkest shadows you ever imagined. Is that all I get? This alone should light a spark and fuel me with anger, injustice, frustration, even. But it doesn't. I'm just sitting here with the dull ache that has accompanied me each minute since I escaped those dark days.

I've watched enough movies to realize other emotions are just as strong. No need to test them all. Imagine if I sensed just one, though? Surely, then, I could focus on the rest? Perhaps I needed to start off smaller. I imagined scenarios that would incite feelings and tried to figure out how I fitted into the equation. Willing to take any chances or risks to give myself the best possible opportunity. To actually participate in each moment and not simply imagine how I'm supposed to act.

I started with suffering and thought hard. What kind of scenario would cause me the most pain? The closest I've ever been was watching the sorrow on your face the day Dad left us. But even this memory is my *imagining* of your hurt. The emotions were never mine.

I required an experience that would affect me and only me. So that I wouldn't need to create or imagine for someone else, but to experience the physical effects, myself.

I started out small at first, digging my nails into my thighs. I had read on a self-harming forum that my upper legs would be the easiest place to hide. For weeks, I dug my nails into my skin, until red raw marks would appear, but I sensed nothing. One time I pushed so hard, I drew blood. I urged anticipation to flood through me, but as the bright red liquid flowed down my thigh and seeped onto the floor; I felt nothing. Empty. Researching the forum voraciously, I had witnessed others' testimony of how much release it gave them, but this wasn't to be my solution. It didn't work for me. Occasionally, when my nails are really long, I double check to see if I'm still unaffected. Pushing them into my thighs until my fingertips became numb.

Accepting that pain would not be the emotion to *unlock me*, my next choice was fear. Little did I know, an occasion was about to present itself. An opportunity to test out my willingness to succumb to my feelings. To put myself at risk because honestly, what do I even have left to lose?

Dear Mom, I'm sorry

Chapter 6

Last June just as school prepared to break for the summer holidays, Jessica Treep held her annual camp out party. She invited everyone in our class, but I knew the invites were simply courtesy and I wasn't actually supposed to accept. In fact, I could think of nothing worse. In what I can only describe as a very sadistic fashion, I began imagining how absolutely awful it would be if I turned up. During my daydreaming, I envisioned myself being embarrassed and out of place. Imagining myself feeling hurt and scared. Yes... this could be it.

I worried you wouldn't let me attend, and so I asked Hannah how best to approach you. "Leave it to me sis, I got you." Hannah's voice reassured me down the line. Later that evening, she face-timed us and we all chatted. Innocently, she asked if I intended to take part in the traditional end-of-year camp out and I feigned disinterest. She immediately commenced a full-on monologue of her experience from only 3 years earlier. She urged you to insist that I attend. That it was a rite of passage. By the time the call ended, you were already compiling a list of things I would require. I hadn't even needed to ask. Hannah really knows how to manipulate you. Watch out for her!

Two weeks later, you dropped me off at the Treep's farm with my tent and overnight backpack. Passing me an extra vinyl bag in which you had packed me some *midnight snacks* and a few bottles of water. I cringed. The others would mock me once I unpacked my goods. Mrs. Treep met us in the driveway and waved you off as she directed me towards the back field where some tents were already erected.

Slowly and reluctantly, I walked towards a group of girls near the tents. I waited for my heart to pound, my mouth dry to the point that the skin in the corners of my lips would flake off, but nope, I felt nothing. I had no doubts; It would be an evening of teasing and being made fun of. If things got bad enough, maybe fear would set in? If I got lucky.

"Jess, who is that?" I heard a blond girl *whisper*. All five heads turned towards me. The O shaped mouth on Jessica's face was picture perfect. I wish I had the guts to snap a picture so I could have shown you later and we would laugh at how uncomfortable she was to see me there at her party. Her looks of disdain informed me, my attendance was not appreciated.

I heard her sharp intake of breath as she approached me. "Ummm, hey, it's Chelsie, right?" I was surprised she knew my name. Nodding towards her, my face contorted into a grimace as I awkwardly smiled in her direction. "Right, I had no idea you would be joining us, but listen why don't you pitch your tent further behind ours?" She waved her hand towards the back of the field. "Let us know if you need anything." She called back over her shoulder as she walked away to rejoin her friends. She must have been making faces or rolling her eyes. I heard the other four girls dissolve into laughter as she sauntered towards them.

I hauled my stuff towards the back of the field and prepared my site. Having never pitched a tent before, I read through the instructions feeling confident I could do it. Over the next couple of hours, another dozen girls arrived, and they all helped each other to set up their tents. After a few mishaps, I finally finished setting up my small orange and gray shelter as Jessica's dad, Bryan, called us over for food.

He had set up a BBQ stand and had a selection of meats and salads on offer. I joined the girls, but remained on the fringes of their circle. I recognized a few of them from school, but the others were Jessica's sports friends or local farm girls. They chatted excitedly about horses and show competitions they had entered recently.

I looked awkward just standing there, kind of listening but not joining in. The boys arrived from the south field to join us. Their presence allowed me to fade into the background. The girls were tossing their hair and laughing exaggeratively, trying to catch the boys' attention. They forgot I was even there. I found a space at one of the long picnic tables and sat down.

There were 5 tables set out, which meant I didn't need to sit too close to anyone. As the other tables filled, a few girls were forced to join my empty table. I sensed they didn't want to sit next to me, but also didn't want to be so obviously rude in front of Jess's parents. A brown-haired girl named Nicole slid down closer to me and then immediately threw her right leg over the bench, facing Debbie on her opposite side. I continued to eat as her back faced me like a barricade, shielding the others.

Focusing on my meal, I listened to their gossiping. A plate piled high with food was placed on the table before me. Looking up, I met the gaze of a freckled-faced boy with brown hair as he sat opposite me. "Hi, I'm James." He announced shyly. The others hadn't heard or chose to ignore him and continued with their own conversations.

"Hi, I'm Chelsie." I gave him a half smile. He had short hair which looked a little frizzy in this humidity. If he put some gel in it, it might fall in perfect little half curls, but clearly, he ran a brush through it and then tried to dampen down the frizz. He was obviously as out of place as I was. "Do you go to our school?" I had never seen him around before. He didn't look familiar.

"No, I'm Jessie's 2nd cousin. My family is here visiting from Kentucky." He informed me proudly. He seemed comfortable, completely oblivious to how out of place he was. Or perhaps, like me, he just didn't care. We talked sporadically for the 20 minutes we stayed at the picnic tables until Karen, (Mrs. Treep) called us for games.

Everyone lined up and Bryan gave us a number when he walked past us. After each person had been given a number, we needed to form into our groups. I had been given number 5, and I headed toward the back of the line to join the other number 5 team members. I approached the small group, relieved I didn't recognize anyone from school. There were 4 boys and 2 girls so far. One girl wouldn't stop whining. She needed to be on team 2 with her friend Kimberly. Her nasally voice was both shrill and annoying. I spotted one boy rolling his eyes at her. This might not be as bad as I thought, I reassured myself. The last member of our team to join us was James. He smiled, slightly nervous, and blushed when he came over to join us. I looked away, not wanting to encourage him.

We played various 5-minute games over the next two hours. I learned from a young age that not having feelings is actually a plus in competitive situations. I don't get nervous or over think, I simply concentrate on the task at hand, so overall I'm a good team member. During Water Balloon dodgeball, I was the last girl left against 4 boys. I might have beaten all four of them, but sensed the other girls didn't appreciate me receiving such attention from the boys. I quickly stepped to my left to ensure the next balloon hit me right in the shin, eager to no longer be the focus of their stares.

Our team almost won the relay cup races, but I purposely stumbled to allow Jessica's team to take the lead. My other team mates were disappointed, but it was easier to let them down than bear the wrath of Jessica and her friends for the rest of the evening.

After the games were finished, everyone was in high spirits and Karen informed us Bryan was setting up a bonfire. "Go get in your jammies and we'll see you back here in half an hour." She smiled.

I trailed behind the other girls towards our makeshift campground in the field. They went into their tents in groups of twos and threes until I was the only one left. I walked the last twenty steps toward my tent slowly, wondering if I might just turn in for the evening and skip the bonfire.

My plan hadn't worked. Although I certainly wasn't welcomed into the group, no one was acting hostile towards me. In fact, some boys, even high-five'd me during the games. I laid out on my sleeping bag and closed my eyes. Willing myself to imagine how it would feel to be part of a team. A group. I envisioned myself smiling back, happy to be included, yet still, I felt nothing. My breath was slow and steady. I pondered staying there until morning, but I heard voices nearing my tent.

"Shhh, I know what to say, c'mon...." Quiet giggles ensued.

"Chelsie? Chelsie, are you there?" Jessica's fake syrupy voice called out. Unzipping the mesh netting, I peeped my head out. It had gotten dark quickly. "There you are!" Jess fake smiled at me. "We thought you might like to walk down to the bonfire with us." She nudged the redhead next to her.

"Yeah, we can all walk down together." The red head agreed. I looked from one to the other and saw another four girls milling in the background. Something was amiss, but I wasn't sure what exactly. Maybe Karen had forced Jessica to come and check on me?

"I'll just grab my sweater." I replied and headed back into my tent. Hastily, I grabbed my long socks and a hoodie, returning to join the others.

We headed towards the bonfire and the girls passed around a tall steel flask. The red-haired girl passed it to me with a raised eyebrow, challenging me to wimp out. I inhaled the scent from the flask; it smelled fiery and sweet with a hint of cinnamon. I took a small swig and passed it back to her. She shook her head at me. "Really. Did you even taste that? That's not a full shot. C'mon all the rest of us have done it. Take a proper chug." She crossed her arms, defying me. I closed my eyes and took a long swallow of the sweet liquid. Within milliseconds, my throat felt as though it was on fire. I started coughing and spluttering. The girls all laughed and taunted me with names like lightweight and little miss perfect.

Ignoring them, I slowed my pace so I that I was near the group but no longer with them. When we reached the bonfire, they quickly joined the boys, and I was left awkwardly on the outskirts of the circle. I spotted James sitting on the far side of the bonfire. He inclined his head toward the empty space available next to him. I didn't really want to sit there, but at least on the other side, I would be far from Jessica and her friends. Reluctantly, I joined him.

"I like your onesie." I searched his features for signs of sarcasm, but his caramel eyes softened as he took in my face, his admiration was genuine. I had my tiger onesie on, complete with tail. As soon as I exited my tent, I knew I was out of place. All the other girls had skimpy cute short sets on or lace edged night dresses and I looked about five in my silly pajamas.

"Grrrr." My attempted growl sounded cringy, even to my own ears, but James laughed whole heartedly.

"Thanks, you too." I stumbled. "I mean, your outfit also looks cool." He had some kind of Anime top on with silky bottoms. It was almost as if he were dressed in cosplay. He was unusual. Weirdly at ease with himself for such a bizarre boy.

One of the blond good-looking boys began strumming a guitar to the opening bars of American Pie. It didn't take long before the whole group joined in. We spent hours singing around the campfire and making s'mores. James toasted me the perfect marshmallows. Golden brown, not burned on the outside, but gooey and melted in the middle. He passed them to me until I took the skewer from his hand and threw it into the grass behind us. "No more." I mouthed silently, wagging my finger at him. He glanced back in the direction where I had launched the skewer and then back to me, surprised. I laughed and leaned towards him. The alcohol had made me a little woozy and I might even have joined in a bit of the singalong.

When it was over and time to head back to our tents, I stumbled as I lifted myself from the ground. James held out a hand to help me steady myself. "Thanks, I must have been sitting too long." I attempted to explain. I was slightly dizzy. His hand felt clammy, however I was grateful for the support. My eyes met his as I released his hand. "No problem, I'm happy to walk you back to your tent, if you wish." His cheeks were flame red. I was not entirely sure if it was from the heat of the fire or from holding my hand. Either way, under the moonlight, he looked endearing. He half shrugged with his palms up, eager to demonstrate he was no threat.

He was simply trying to be friendly; I hadn't had a friend in a long time. Why not allow him to accompany me? At least then I would be spared Jessica and her tribe ribbing me. "Sure, thanks." I accepted shyly.

On the short walk back to my tent, James told me about his horse, Granger, back in Kentucky. His family owned a large farm, and he worked as a ranch hand after school and weekends. He was an A+ student, not because he loved school but because he didn't love ranching. He wanted to make sure he could get into law at Harvard, so he would no longer be available to help at home. "Can't you just tell your family it's not really your thing? Explain to them that you don't really enjoy it?" I asked him.

Shaking his head, he continued walking, his gaze focused towards the ground. "It's in my dad's blood. Four generations of Carter's have owned farmland in Kentucky. It would break his heart if he thought I didn't love it." His voice was soft, fragile even. In its sorrow, I heard all the things he wasn't saying. For the first time in years, I felt a connection to someone. James was trying to live his life without hurting his family or disappointing them. If anyone understood that, it was me.

I slipped my hand into his, reassuring him, he was not alone. I wanted to see how it felt. His hand was cool but soft. He glanced at me nervously. I smiled back at him shyly. He tightened his grip as we walked the rest of the way in silence. The stars illuminated the sky. It was the perfect romantic scene, except for us. Neither of us belonged in this backdrop.

Upon arrival at my tent, we stood facing each other awkwardly. I could hear the other girls heading towards their tents now and wanted to be out of the way before they got closer. "Do you want a midnight snack?" I offered. "My mom packed me a goodie bag and I'll never eat them all by myself." I gestured towards the tent and my eyes glanced furtively down the field as the girls' voices came closer.

He nodded. The pink blush crept back into his cheeks. I don't think he trusted himself to speak. We quickly entered the tent, eager to hide before we were spotted by Jessica and her entourage. With no moonlight inside, it took a few seconds for our eyes to adjust to the dark. I found my backpack and turned on my small battery-operated camping lamp. It was too bright, so I placed my t-shirt over it. A soft glow filled the tent. I piled all the snacks in the middle of my sleeping bag and we picked our favorites, one by one.

I chose the red licorice first and James grabbed the gummy worms. We both picked a cream egg as our second choice. We continued until there were only the mini dark chocolate bars that neither of us wanted.

James smiled mischievously as he pulled a small tin out of his pocket. He unscrewed its cap and offered it in my direction. Small sugar covered jellies in bright vivid colors beckoned me. My brow furrowed, and I tilted my head. "They're just gummies." His raised eyebrows taunting me to try one.

I had heard about edibles, but never experimented with them myself. "Actually, I'm already on some pretty heavy prescription medication, so I'm going to have to pass." My nose crinkled in a childlike way. My cheeks burned bright red. It was hot in there with just the two of us and no air circulating.

We chatted effortlessly for more than an hour. He asked me so many questions about our family and I encouraged him to describe in detail to me how he was feeling as his gummy kicked in. James was easy to be with. I felt nothing having him there in the tent with me. I wasn't concerned anyone would find him. I wasn't worried about what he thought about me. It was all just fine. In that moment, being there with him, I was fine. I wondered if I let him kiss me. Would it be the fireworks everyone speaks of in movies and books? As he talked about his school life back home, I closed my eyes and imagined what it would be like. When I opened my eyes, James was staring at me. "You're really beautiful, Chelsie. I bet guys are always telling you that." Clearly, James couldn't read social gestures any better than I could. Had he not noticed all evening that I was on the outskirts of the group? Tolerated but not welcomed?

I kneeled towards him. "Thanks. No guy has ever said that to me before." I gently leaned forward and pressed my lips against his. I wasn't sure how to kiss someone, but his lips were dry, so I tried a few soft little kisses. Slowly, he reached his hand around my neck and gently pulled me further forward. He parted his lips and kissed me gently.

Rolling over onto his side, he made room for me to lie down beside him and we continued kissing. His kisses grew eager, his hands slowly caressed my back. His breath came in short, shallow gasps, as though he needed more oxygen. I knew I should feel some kind of excitement, trepidation or fear even, but I felt nothing. I wasn't uncomfortable, and the kissing was ok, but it had sparked no feelings. After a while, I laid my head against his chest and he continued the circle motions on my back. We talked long into the night, discovering our similarities and differences. James kept describing the sensation of his gummy and I closed my eyes, imagining I was floating in its effects too. Eventually we fell asleep, just like that. Two outcasts, together as one.

Chapter 7

In the morning I woke hot and sweaty as the sun's intense heat made it through the thin nylon of my tent. I wriggled a little, hoping to wake James with my movement. "Good morning." His voice sounded hoarse. He cleared his throat. "Did you sleep ok?"

I sat up and smiled at him. "Yeah, I slept great, thanks." I hadn't really, the ground was too hard. My little foam mattress had not been big enough for the both of us. His smile beamed back at me, relieved. I had slept well and enjoyed our night together. Obviously, this was his first experience with a girl. I didn't want him to regret it, like he didn't do a good job. It wasn't his fault. I was inept, unable to reciprocate any emotion. If I could, I would probably really like James. His easy-going attitude and shy smile were nice. It was comfortable to be with him.

We agreed he would run back to his tent before anyone else woke up and I would see him later at breakfast. He kissed my forehead tenderly. "See you later sweet Chelsie." He rubbed my cheeks with his thumb as though taking a mental picture of me.

"Thanks for a great night, James." I replied. I wanted to help him feel good about himself. Despite not having felt anything, I could tell James was feeling enough for the both of us. He disappeared silently out of the tent and I lay there quietly, listening to his footsteps as they faded.

Isn't physical attraction supposed to be the greatest feeling? People long for one another with desire soaring through their bodies, except mine. Is it my mind or my body that's broken? My mind knows what and how I'm supposed to feel, so is it my body that can't do it or my brain that can't send the right transmitters? I wish I knew. It's like, if I could just figure out what exactly about me is broken then I might have more chance to fix it, right?

I gathered my towel and a change of clothes and headed towards the main house to get ready for the day. Passing the other girl's tents, I tiptoed as quietly as possible, ensuring not to wake them. Perfect. I could get showered, dressed, and ready to go while they remained sleeping.

I approached the pool house wash rooms and let myself in. Three curtains divided the shower stalls and two were already running. I stepped into the third one at the end and turned on the faucet. The water massaged my sore body from sleeping on the hard ground and I closed my eyes, letting the heat do its work. Vaguely aware of the two female voices chatting, but I wasn't listening to them.

I showered quickly. I didn't want to take too long in case others might be waiting so as soon as I rinsed the conditioner out of my hair, I turned the taps off.

"Well, I saw him creeping away from her tent this morning. I guess she's more exciting than we thought." I recognized Amber's voice from my history class at school. They had seen James. I slowly dried myself, willing them to be gone by the time I exited the stall.

"Just goes to show. It's always the quiet ones." Jessica roared at her own joke. It sounded as if they were gathering their things from the sink counter. Their voices drifted as they walked away from the pool house. I waited a few moments after they left before pulling back the shower curtain.

My face appeared flush in the mirror. Bright pink cheeks from the heat of the water. I tried to look at myself as James had. Large green eyes stared back at me above a small pert nose and full pink lips. My mousy brown hair softly tousled around my shoulders, neither straight nor curly. I smiled at my reflection, urging myself to find beauty. I looked fine, not pretty, not beautiful, just fine.

I applied some lotion to my face and a light lip gloss. I threw my hair in a high ponytail and set off in search of breakfast.

The picnic tables were full. Grabbing a plate, I filled it with some fruit salad, a bagel, and scrambled eggs from the buffet table. Bryan and Karen must have been up all morning preparing it.

A few boys wanted to play volleyball before they left and were already vacating their table. I slid into one bench near the end, away from everyone else. James appeared out of nowhere, joining me. At once, I heard giggles from Amber's table as she and Jessica elbowed the other girls around them to check us out.

I ignored them; I had years of practice. Poor James, not used to such an audience, looked at me startled. The redness of his neck traveled all the way up his face. Leaving him looking like a startled beetroot.

He asked me about my plans for the week, and I fabricated a story about going to visit Hannah at school for the next few days. He seemed a nice boy, but I didn't want to meet him again. What was the point? He offered me his cell number, and I reassured him I would keep in touch. Finishing my breakfast, I explained I needed to gather my things together, that I would get picked up soon. Disappointment cast a shadow across his cheery freckled face, but I was doing my best to let him down gently. I stood and brushed the toast crumbs off my denim shorts. "It's been great to meet you James, stay in touch ok?" I stated casually as I cleaned my plate and cutlery from the table.

He looked confused and a little crushed. "Yeah you too, Chelsie. I'll text you!" He promised as I walked away.

Hearing the odd word through the whispers and giggles of the other girls didn't affect me. This experience permitted me to subject myself to new situations and opportunities. Allowing myself to be vulnerable, open to the possibility of being dejected and hurt. I was disappointed it didn't work, but at least I had tried. I had accomplished what I set out to do.

Heading back towards my camping spot, I walked quickly with purpose. Within thirty minutes, I had packed away my things. I was ready, and you were on your way to pick me up.

On my walk towards the drive to wait for you, Jessica and Amber called out to me. "Bye Chelsie, glad you had such a great time!" Waving my hand in the air, I didn't even glance back at them. I knew from their sniggering they were mocking me yet again. I got what I needed out of this, even if I didn't get what I hoped for.

You pulled up onto the gravel driveway, your face bright with excitement. "Hi, honey, how was it? Did you have a good time? Was it a late night? Did you have enough snacks?"

I'm used to you filling the silence with your worrisome questions. "I had fun, Mom. Everything was fine." I placed my hand on your forearm to reassure you, I'm ok, nothing happened. We drove home amicably, singing along to songs on the radio. The creases on your forehead faded and your grip on the steering wheel loosened. Your mind, literally unwinding. I had taken part in a party and I came home fine. Maybe I had even enjoyed myself. You could relax now.

However, my insides were heavier than before. Putting myself out there; had changed nothing. Fear, excitement, and even desire had eluded me. The sleepover had just confirmed what I already learned. No matter how hard I tried or how many new experiences I subjected myself to, I would be stuck pretending forever. The only thing I had actually achieved was to make a friend, but honestly, I didn't even want the friendship. Just one more person I have to act for. Although that's unfair of me because James never asked me to be someone I'm not and his own candor and honesty concerning his home life encouraged me to be as honest as I dared with him.

When I arrived home and unpacked my bag, I discovered James' little tin of gummies. He must have dropped them in my bag last night. Later that evening, my phone pinged while we ate dinner at the table. I picked it up and read the message. 'I had a great time. I realize you couldn't really let go, but if ever you want a little help, I left my tin in your bag for you.' Smiling, I sent back a laughing emoji. Three little dots played on the screen until he hit send, 'Day or night, Chelsie. I am here for you. Expecting nothing in return ok?' I reread his words, multiple times, unsure how to reply. Feeling brave, I texted back. 'I'm going to hold you to that, James!' My face must have given me away, as you and Ben both stared at me when I raised my gaze from the screen.

"Anything interesting happening on your phone there, Chelsie?" You teased me.

"Yeah, spill the tea, Chels." Ben chimed in. I caught your eye and we both burst out laughing at Ben's eagerness to join in the gossip. I slipped my phone into my pocket and regaled the two of you with stories of singing around the campfire and my *almost* win at dodgeball. The distraction proved successful. You never followed up or asked who I was texting so I never needed to explain. Distraction and evasion, two of my best tactics to avoid adding to the never-ending list of lies.

Most of my communication with James is now via email. He sends me regular updates on Kentucky life and I send him my thoughts, my worries. It's been more than a year now and we're still some kind of friends, so the *experiment* wasn't a complete loss. I've kept James a secret all this time. I wonder if there's something wrong with that? I spend so much of my time lying, but the best friends I have are a secret from everyone. I don't want to lie about James or Luke. It would seem disloyal to them.

Isn't this ironic? I know in my mind what disloyalty is but my heart fails me once again.

Dear Mom, I'm sorry

Chapter 8

My mind whirls a lot. Having spent most of my life observing my surroundings and the people in it, sometimes it's like I have too many thoughts. It's the making sense of everything. I'm not just observing other people, I'm actively studying them, their reactions, their outcomes. Some things trigger certain people while others are unaffected. Some yell, others sulk, the smart ones walk away. It's hard trying to figure out who are the best people to copy. Who I should be like. Of course, Hannah was my go-to reference, but she didn't appreciate me copying her. Sometimes, the thoughts become so jumbled and confused in my mind, I can't interpret or study anything. I seek the privacy of my room to unscramble the mess when it becomes overwhelming.

When I was younger, I would scribble. Watching the jumbled thoughts leave my brain and end up in a mess on the paper. This became kind of therapeutic for me. You would find scribbled papers under my bed and ask me what they were. I didn't have the words or the capability to explain them to you. I would just smile and say "nice". You would move the paper in your hand in different positions, trying to visualize something that wasn't there. I tapped the fridge door, wanting you to put my art on display like Hannah's pretty flower painting she brought home from school that week.

You smoothed out the paper scrap and placed it under a magnet on the fridge. I clapped my hands and smiled, eager to show you I liked my work on the fridge just like Hannah.

Several times that week, I would find you facing the fridge, looking at my scrap art. At first, I assumed you really liked it, but the confused look on your face and the slight shake of your head as you snapped out of your daze informed me otherwise. You couldn't make sense of it.

To me it was a reminder that my mind was capable of staying clear. Releasing all my thoughts on the paper, I didn't have to keep the chaos inside of me. For you, it was something else. A constant reminder of how different I was. That something about me wasn't quite right, and it made you sad. I stopped asking for my scribbles to be placed on the fridge. I never wanted you to be sad. I tried to make fewer scribbles, to keep the jumble in my brain instead, where you wouldn't see it, where it wouldn't make you sad anymore.

When I was six, you bought me a Spiro-graph for Christmas. I placed the pen in the little hole and turned it in all directions. Now I no longer had scribbles. I had perfect geometric drawings. After I had tested it out, you clapped your hands together excitedly. "Oh my goodness, Hannah. Come and see this art Chelsie has made." Reluctantly, Hannah left her Barbie Dream House to come and see my work.

"Good job, Chels. Now you can make nice scribbles." Hannah encouraged. I looked at her questioningly. Surely, Hannah understood me better? She rolled her eyes and winked at me as she walked past. Reassuring me, it was easier to humor you.

Dear Mom, I'm sorry

I drew accurate little circles all day, and you taped at least five of them to the fridge. You and Dad even had a vote on which one was best. The drawings were deliberate shapes. They didn't clear my jumbled mind.

That night, I took my Snoopy magic slate board that I received in my stocking to bed with me. I smoothed down the plastic covering with my hand. Removing the hard red pencil from its transparent casing, I applied it to the magnetic plastic. Slowly, I started drawing circles, whirling together like my thoughts. The more I drew, the lighter my mind became. When I ran out of space, I held the little board in my hand until I fell asleep.

In the morning, I woke still clenching my scribbled pad. I lifted the thin plastic sheet and gently peeled it back, slowly erasing all my scribbles, making the page clean again. I tucked it in under my pillow to use again that night.

From that Christmas onwards, every year, I received gifts that were art based. Replacing my scribbles with the spirograph made you perceive things as more organized. More in control.

One year you even bought me those little wooden building logs. The ones where kids build cabins out of. I spent hours building the perfect model and once everything was exactly right, I would knock it over. Watching all the logs fall to the floor, all my hard work erased in seconds. While I was building, my mind would run frantically. Should I go taller or wider? Windows or doors? So many options and so many choices. Once it was built, I would survey it. I should definitely have made the windows wider. They looked too small. The door way barely fit my little hand through it. As soon as I knocked it, my mind stopped. Peace descended on me and I was relaxed.

Your face would be crestfallen as you rushed into the room. "Oh no, Chelsie! Did your logs fall over?" You enquired. I would nod at you, smiling. I can still remember the emotion. It's what I envisioned happiness felt like. "Let me help you. We can rebuild." Your tone reassuring me, everything would be all right. Gathering all the logs together, you quickly placed them in order and my sense of peace would be lost.

Sadly, I wandered to my room whilst you put the logs away. "Poor Chelsie," I heard you whisper to Dad. "She always ends up wrecking her buildings. Maybe I should get her fine motor skills tested again?" Eventually, you stopped getting the logs out. When I asked for them, you would direct my interest elsewhere. "How about these Lego? They click together and don't fall down. Those are better aren't they?" Nodding your head with a wide smile, eager for me to enjoy the Lego and the structure they might bring to my playing. They weren't better. I hated them, but it made you happy when I was creating something that couldn't be destroyed.

Now at fifteen, I'm enrolled in online Art Classes I dread attending. When the instructor sends out a list of materials needed for the week ahead, you rush out to buy everything I'll need.

You confer with me, "are these pencils better than those other ones you have?" I long to tell you, I don't care and to put an end to the façade, but your crumpled disappointed face haunts me from previous times when I tried the truth. Whoever said the truth will set you free, lied. The truth just takes the jumbled-up scribbles from your mind and puts them on the table for everyone to sift through and have an opinion on. The truth hurts other people and confuses them.

You've spent my entire life searching for the right programs to enroll me in. The right therapy to help support me. Concluding that these solutions are working, that I'm getting *better* helps you to maintain the status quo. With Hannah away at Uni and Ben soon entering puberty, you don't need another child to worry about. You need a break. You need a *best Mom* sticker. My way of giving you all that is continuing the art classes. Pretending I love art as much as you assume I do.

The dry erase board on my desk has replaced my old abused magic slate. Its hard little red pencil has been upgraded with markers, all the colors of the rainbow. Sometimes when I doodle my thoughts nowadays, I'll even color code them. I use blue when I think of Ben. Purple for Hannah. Red for you. Yellow for Luke. I don't need to quieten my mind since I'm on my meds because my thoughts don't race anymore. Sometimes when I close my eyes tight, I imagine I can remember that old sensation and I try to stay in the moment as long as I can, even if it's only seconds. To remember that nice quiet moment in my mind. Not the emptiness that I feel now, but the peace I enjoyed then.

Dear Mom, I'm sorry

Chapter 9

This weekend I've arrived to spend a week with Dad and Melanie. I attempted to skip it, especially as Ben wasn't coming, but you reminded me that dad only gets to see me twice a year and it wasn't fair to cut out his visits.

The real difficulty is you remember Dad the way he was when you were married. The dad who didn't leave us to have an affair with his secretary. Who looked after his family when times got tough. I'm not sure if that person ever existed or just in your mind, but I can attest that man is not the dad I have to visit. I have tried to explain it to you after other visits, but you're so adamant to be a good parent and not trash talk dad, you can't really hear me.

As soon as my cell phone gets service on my arrival in Fort Myers, my phone vibrates. 'Hey girl! Your dad and I are running a little late. Grab a coffee at the espresso bar and we'll be there as soon as we can. Can't wait to see you!' Rolling my eyes, I stuff my phone back into my jacket pocket, grab my weekend bag from the overhead compartment and make my way off the plane.

I find an empty table at the espresso bar and order a Snapple. I can't believe Melanie suggested coffee. Have you ever seen me drink coffee? Like ever? She knows zilch about me. I pull out my phone and scroll through Tik Toks while I wait for them to arrive. They only live twenty minutes away, so I am expecting them to be fairly soon.

"There you are, Chelsie." Dad jovially approaches my table, an hour later, as though I was the one who had been missing. He's dressed in white shorts and a polo shirt. Melanie is also dressed very sporty, in a tennis skirt with a pink mesh tank top.

"How have you been? We're so excited to see you!" Melanie exclaims as she leans down and hugs me. Her perfume overwhelms my senses and I hold my breath to avoid drowning in its overpowering scent. I try not to talk to you about Melanie. I don't like to remind you of those painful days when you first discovered her existence. The truth is, I hate

Melanie. Her beady little eyes and upturned nose remind me of a rat. Her fake over exuberant voice shrills through my ears. Dad loves it. He's so happy looking at her all proud like she's ever achieved anything in her life. Her fake smiles are wasted on me. Observing people my entire life has allowed me to read people and I know a calculating bitch when I see one. Driving back to their condo on the beach, they fill me in on their morning at the country club where they had been playing tennis. So, that's why they were late. I stare out the window as we leave Fort Myers and concentrate on the scenery. They could have played tennis any day of the year in sunny Florida, but the morning of my arrival seemed the perfect convenient time for them. The drive to Elmwood passes quickly, I distract my mind counting palm trees. I count 47 by the time we reach dad's house.

Once I finish unpacking, Melanie asks if I would like to lie out by the pool. I had discovered early on that Melanie likes to *show* dad, what a great mother figure she is to me. It's far easier to pretend I'm addicted to being in the pool and working on my year-round tan, than to hang around them and their school crush behavior.

When the weather is nice, I can spend more than half of my time down by the pool and away from them. Melanie doesn't like dad to sit in the sun, because of the dangers of skin cancer, so they'll leave me alone down there. I dig out one of my new swimsuits from the bottom drawer and try it on. It's jet black, with fluorescent patches sewn in through the mesh to cover any *private* areas. On the mannequin in the store, it looked fun and frivolous. As I study my image in the floor-length mirror, I'm now very unsure. The sides are cut high, accentuating my long, slim legs. The bust area provides just enough support to create a sensual cleavage, which peaks through the sheer mesh. Gathered tucks around my buttocks make my butt look full and lifted. I thought I should try something different for once. Attempt to look like the girls at the beach, but now that I do, I realize I look wrong. I would never go to a public beach in this. Boys would stare as their eyes silently devoured my curves. The mean girls would whisper that I was an attention seeking ho. Reaching for the coverup, hanging off the hook on the back of the door, I throw it on. That's better. I nod at my reflection. The sheer polyester successfully hides any shape my body may have underneath.

The irony is not lost on me. I might feel nothing, but even my clothes hold the power to incite emotions from others. Pulling my long hair into a messy bun, I pop my sunglasses on top of my head. You packed my favorite oversized towel for me and I inhale its scent deeply. Notes of lavender fill my nostrils, a familiar smell of home. I grab my Airpods from the bedside table and head back towards the kitchen.

"All settled in, Kiddo?" Dad asks as he notices me approach. I smile at him in affirmation. I know he's uncomfortable. He doesn't know how to talk to me. He's afraid of saying or doing the wrong thing and therefore just regularly checks in that I'm ok. Usually, Ben is here with me and it's easier, less strained. Currently, it's a lose-lose situation. Dad doesn't know what to say to me and Melanie has a gift for saying the wrong thing.

For a split second, I imagine admitting to him the truth. I'm not ok now and never will be in the future. My days are numbered now and I am simply in a countdown. Would he gather me in his arms and reassure me that together we will find a way? Or would I have to watch his face crumple in fear and despair? To see the haunting worry that veils his eyes whenever he looks in my direction. I catch his furtive look towards Melanie. It's his 'get me out of here' look. I know it well. My inability to feel has advantages in that I am an avid observer and pick up on body language and subtleties that others never notice. It's like my superpower. I can't feel but I can see clearly what others feel. Sometimes even better than they can themselves.

"So, your dad and I are just going to pop into the club while you're hanging out at the pool. We don't wanna cramp your style, do we, Chris?" Her fake shrill laugh echoes through the large open plan layout of the living area. Dad stands up from the couch and stretches as though awakening himself to the idea of going out. Although I know damn well, he's been itching to leave since I've arrived.

Honestly Mom, how did you even stay married to him? He's such a flake. Obsessed with his tennis game and his 30-year-old wife's physique. He doesn't even seem to care that she's devoid of any substantial thoughts of her own. I glance in her direction. She's pouting in the hallway mirror as she smacks her lips together having applied her lip gloss. Catching my stare for just a millisecond, a look of disdain crosses her eyes before she plasters another fake smile across her over made-up face. "Let's go Chris, we don't wanna be late! There are leftovers from last night's take out in the fridge, Chelsie, help yourself." She waves towards the fridge in case I've forgotten where it is. Dad shrugs on his windbreaker and nods in my direction, again checking if I'm ok.

"Have fun, you two!" I call out, making my way towards the patio doors. I don't glance back, but the latch of the door clicking confirms they've left. I choose a lounger in the full sun to have a nap. During most of my week here, I will be alone. Dad and Melanie will constantly pop out, only to text me a few hours later asking if I need anything. When I decline, their follow-up message will suggest that I order food or grab something from one of the food trucks down by the promenade. It's a silly façade. They don't really want me here. They have no idea what to do with me, so they'll spend their entire week avoiding me. I wish Ben was here. Maybe this is what it feels like to miss someone. The idea that time will drag by slower. Feeling numb, I press play on my summer vibes list and close my eyes from the blinding sun.

෨෧

I'm at the park playing fetch with Luke. I'm on top of a small hill, throwing the ball as Luke runs happily after it. His golden hair flying in the wind as saliva excitedly sneaks from his mouth. He catches the tennis ball and turns eagerly to find me. The ascent is nice and steep, helping him to use some of that energy he seems to have today. He's not normally like this. So excited and free. I guess I've never really seen him outside of his front yard before. It seems weird being with him here. I don't understand how we arrived and I don't think I've ever been to this park before. I can sense how happy Luke is, and it makes me feel warm inside.

I lie down on the grass and Luke snuggles up to me. He curls into a ball beside me. I pet his soft, silky head and he lifts it to meet my gaze. "You're safe here with me." I reassure him. He licks my cheek before tucking his snout into his hind legs. A low sigh escapes him as he releases his breath. His stomach rises and falls in a slow rhythm as he drifts off to sleep. I drape an arm around him as I lay my hand with his front paw, closing my eyes. Listening to the sound of his breathing.

༄ঌ

Something's vibrating next to me. My eyes dart open, worried that Luke is hurt. My phone! It's my phone that's vibrating. I'm on the lounger by the pool at Dad's and Melanie's. Luke isn't here. I'm not at the park, I never was. I read the text that so rudely awakened me from my dream.

'Hey kiddo, we're just gonna grab some food here at the club. We shouldn't be too late but if you're already asleep when we get home, I'll see you in the morning x.' It's from Dad, I mean I guess I should be grateful that he's bothered to text me and not just got Melanie to palm me off as per usual. I feel flat, which is different. Often, I feel numb, but right now I feel flat. Not sure if it's the text or the realization that it was all a dream and Luke is not actually here. Flat feels different to numb. I half smile, not sure if I've actually experienced a feeling but excited to discover more.

I have an urge to go walking, fortunately I know the neighborhood pretty well. Dad has lived here since I was 10, so I've had years of discovering it. When we were younger, Hannah would take Ben and me on little bike rides.

Heading back to the house, I throw on my black mesh shorts and a t-shirt. Haphazardly lacing up my running shoes and grabbing a bottle of water from the fridge, I leave a scribbled note on the counter to say I've gone for a walk, but I'm pretty sure I'll be back before anyone sees it.

Pressing the lock button on the front door, I make my way down the driveway. It's after eight but still bright, so I set off toward the local community park. The subdivision is filled with cookie cutter houses. Bungalows with high windows to allow the sun to stream in and bounce light and color around the rooms. Every single house I pass is a shaded version of beige. I imagine the designer used a color palette termed something like the Sahara dessert. Beiges, warm creams, peachy browns, like they're all the same color but each one different. You know the type, modern but simple. There are roughly 20 streets in the area and they all branch off Ridgeway Drive, which curves in a semicircle through the small subdivision. Right at the center, in the heart of the community, there's a little park with a kids' play area, a BMX track and an off-leash dog park.

I slip onto a lone tire swing hung from a massive great oak tree overlooking the fenced in dog run. There's an older man throwing sticks for his little puppy. He shows the fluffy gray and white puppy the stick and lunges it forward. Confused, the little pup tilts his head from side to side, wondering where the stick has gone. The old man points in the direction towards the stick but the excited puppy continues eagerly attempting to climb his legs in search of treats. Looking disappointed, the owner heads off to pick up the stick and start his game of fetch all over again.

For over thirty minutes, I watch the man and his pup. They are preparing to leave as dusk descends and I decide also to make my way home. The man heads off towards the car park while the fluffy white little fur ball attempts to run in every and any direction at once, only to be pulled back towards his master with a little tug of his leash.

I wish I could tell that puppy not to worry. He'll soon get the hang of it. Watching people, learning what they expect from you. He'll learn how to make his owner happy, eventually. It's hard when you don't understand the same

Dear Mom, I'm sorry

language as everyone else. I understood his confusion to the depth of my bones.

Chapter 10

Today dad is bringing me for a father-daughter day out. I'm sure this is something Melanie arranged to get rid of us for the day. I've had enough of tanning and people watching at the park, at least it will be something different.

Dressed in denim shorts and a short sleeve Care Bears shirt, I head to the kitchen. When I was little, I was fascinated by these cute little bears. Even the grumpy one looked soft and cuddly. You gifted me a Tenderheart bear for my 8th birthday and I carried it everywhere. I secretly wished I was a Care bear. My special power would be giving good feelings to others.

"So do I get a hint, where we are going?" I ask dad as he grabs a couple of bottles of water from the fridge, adding them to our travel bag.

A smirk plays around his lips. "You'll see soon enough."

"I'm not sure anyone would consider a two-hour drive *soon.*" Melanie rolls her eyes at me, and I realize she's not joining us because of the journey. She doesn't like long car rides. It's because she's a control freak. Maybe this wasn't her idea after all?

"I'll have dinner ready for 6'ish. How does that sound, Chris?" She zips up our bag and passes it to dad.

"Don't go to any trouble on our account, Mel, Chelsie and I will play things by ear. We don't want to be tied down to a schedule on our day of adventure. Am I right, Chels?" Dad winks at me and I nod.

"Well, I certainly wouldn't want to interfere with your plans." Her voice is short, her tone curt. She folds her arms across her chest, glaring at dad.

"No worries about that, because we have no actual plans. We're going to go wherever the wind takes us!" Chuckling, he picks up his mobile, adding it to the bag, hanging off his shoulder. He steps toward Melanie and leans down to kiss her forehead. She rocks back on her heels ever so slightly that he almost misses. Her narrowed eyes glaring

at him. Obliviously, he calls out "Later, alligator," and heads
to the front hallway.

A laugh almost escapes me as I watch her annoyance
turn to surprise, shock even. With a small wave, I skip out
to the foyer.

The drive is easy. I take care of the playlist of songs
and dad navigates us through the roads, out of Englewood.
We take highway 75 towards Sarasota and I quickly rack
my brain wondering what attractions are based there that
dad might bring me to. Once passed some minor road works
in Siesta Key, we travel through Sarasota without delay,
heading in the direction of St. Petersburg according to the
overhead signs.

We singalong to old 80s rock tunes until we arrive at
our destination, the Clearwater Marine Rescue Center.

"Dolphins!" I screech out loud and smiling at dad who
is looking pleased with himself, to say the least.

"Not just any dolphins. We're here to meet Hope." Dad
announces proudly as he exits the car.

I unbuckle my seatbelt as fast as I can. "Like my
Hope? Dolphin's Tale Hope?" I demand, catching up with

him, walking towards the entrance. He shrugs his shoulders and rolls his eyes at me.

"Dad, stop messing around." I swat him on the arm and he opens it to pull me in close.

We walk around the aquarium like that for the entire visit. Dad hasn't been here before, but he becomes my personal tour guide for the day. Reading out the displays to me, and hurrying us through the exhibits to catch feeding time with Walle and Boomer, the cutest otters you'll ever meet.

Nothing could have prepared me for my one-on-one experience with Hope. Do you remember when they announced the second movie, and I barely slept for weeks? My Dolphin Tale DVD wouldn't even play anymore. It had so many scratches. I could never love a movie more. At least that's what I thought until the sequel was released and I was mesmerized by Hope.

Instead of a souvenir, Dad purchases a sponsorship package so I can officially adopt Hope, contributing to her well-being. Watching her swim around the tank, jumping in the air and even wetting us with her tail flipping was the highlight of our day.

"Ben, sure will be jellie he missed this." I smile at dad as we walk back to the car just before closing time. You would think 6 hours was enough for anyone, but we would have stayed longer if they let us!

Starting the engine, dad clears his throat and looks at me.

"Last time Ben visited I took him to the game community? Today was something special for you. I'm sorry if it doesn't always seem like I make time for you or understand you better. It was the same with Hannah through her teen years. I'm awkward around teenage girls. I always have been," he laughs. "Ask your mom. She'll tell you all about it." His eyes soften. Without another word, we set course back to Englewood. Slipping my hand casually through his arm, I lean into his shoulder and stay there the entire way home.

Dear Mom, I'm sorry

Chapter 11

Lifting my bag from the carousel, I head towards our meeting point. My DKNY case rolls across the gleaming tiles behind me. Ahead through the glass doors, I see the Chevy at once. That's one advantage of a sky-blue car. It's easy to spot even if it does look like a toy.

"Chelsieeeeeeee, over here, honey." You are literally stretched from the driver's side towards the open passenger window, calling out to me. There are only two other cars parked out front, honestly I wonder how you think I could miss you. I smile and wave back at your excited face.

I hoist my case into the open trunk and shut it down tight. You lean forward to push open the passenger door and I slide into the seat beside you. Your arms reach around and squeeze me so tight. "How was your flight? Are you hungry? I bet you're tired. I put fresh sheets on your bed so you can climb into it as soon as we get back and catch up on your rest."

I shake my head to indicate that I'm neither tired nor hungry, but I can see you're gripped in anxiety as you chatter away, filling the space between us. I nod and *hmmm*, agreeing with your statements. Over the years, you've realized that questions make me uncomfortable so often without realizing it, you answer them yourself as statements.

"I bet that constant heat tired you out every day as well. The heat does that to us all. You know it really drains people." I'm sure it drains people, but not a 15-year-old who has nothing to do all day. But it's easier to nod and agree with you. I encourage your recount of my vacation because if you narrate it, it will be as wonderful as you hoped it would be for me. Should I interrupt or correct you about how it really was. The frown lines on your forehead will crease and the shadows under your eyes will have returned by tomorrow, thanks to another sleepless night spent worrying about me. I never want that for you. The constant worry and stress.

While you navigate the traffic singing along to the radio, I catch a side glance at you. You appear more relaxed than I've seen you in a long time. More at ease with yourself. For a second, I'm wondering if you've had Botox and I'm contemplating asking as you notice my stare.

"What's wrong honey?" Your hand pats my knee in a reassuring gesture. Instantly I see a look of concern replace your easy smile from just seconds ago and in that moment I realize. You didn't have Botox. You had a holiday. You enjoyed a well-deserved break. Now I am back, so is the weight and concern you carry on your shoulders. In that split second, I am so grateful that I can no longer feel, because if I could, I think I would cry.

"Oh, I was just caught in a daze. You're so right. It's exhausting traveling." I convince you and the creases on your forehead smooth out even if the glint of worry is still there in your eyes.

You turn up the volume dial on the radio as the voice of Ed Sheeran croons from the speakers and we sing along the rest of the ride home. It's the happiest I've seen you in so long. When I am gone, I wonder if you will laugh like this again? I sure hope so. I hope the responsibility, worry and fear will eventually subside for you with time and you will regain a life. Maybe I won't be here but instead of us both pretending at half a life each, I'll be at peace and you'll create a life for yourself with Ben and Hannah.

By the time we arrive home, the sun is setting. Ben opens the door as I push my case up the driveway.

"Chelsie, welcome home. I've missed you so much." He throws his arms around me. I love Ben's enthusiasm. He's my favorite person to hang out with. Please tell him that? In years to come, that he helped me hold on, longer than I ever would have without him?

His fast speech and invasion of my personal space allow me to *feel* how much Ben has missed me. He doesn't reign in his feelings like everyone else does around me. His emotions are so big, sometimes I think they're enough for the both of us. If ever I get a glimpse of what feelings are, I get it when I'm with Ben. He feels so fully, almost electric. His laughing, smiling face is all-consuming. He doesn't keep his happiness in shadows or pretend his feelings are less than to make me feel better or whatever the reason is the rest of you all do it. Ben is honestly one of the few people who is still 100% authentic with me, and I regret that you and Hannah could never share true joy with me. Worried your happiness or enjoyment would somehow cast an even larger shadow over my gloomy outlook. Dad does it too. This morning at the airport, I could see how sad he was to say goodbye to me and so Melanie did all the talking.

"Now, we've dropped your bag off. Let's accompany you to the security area." Grabbing dad's arm, she steered him towards the security gates C & D.

Dad nodded towards the coffee bar a little further down the hallway. "Do you want to get a drink before you go through?" He asked quietly. Melanie jerked her neck back towards dad, surprised at his offer. His left leg shook subtly.

"I better go now, just in case they board early." I declined. My flight was still 2 hours away, but the idea of sitting on a hard metal chair waiting and bored still sounded better than another minute with Melanie. Dad nodded despondently. Melanie flung her arm around me, announcing how she couldn't wait 'til I came back again.

Awkwardly, Dad took my hands in his. "I know this trip has not been the best for you without Ben or Hannah but our day out is one of the best I've enjoyed in a long time." I leaned in to hear him. He opened his arms as I bent forward and enveloped me tight in his embrace. I gave him a squeeze to acknowledge that I appreciated the sentiment. Admittedly, he struggles to communicate his feelings, but this was the best he's managed in a long time.

"I love you so much, Chelsie." He murmured into my hair. I pulled away and kissed him softly on the cheek.

"I love you too, Dad." I dropped his hand and turned to join the security line. Melanie dragged him towards the escalators. I quickly looked away as his head turned in my direction. His last memory, shouldn't be of me left alone in that line. I knew that would make him sad. Forcing myself to look back, I coaxed my features into a smile to reassure him. He was subtly wiping his eye as the metal steps descended him from my view into the ground.

After unpacking all of my clothes into the washing machine, you order take-away and we agree Ben can choose the movie tonight. You tilt your head to one side, knowing I'm not the biggest fan of dinosaurs as Ben's hand hovers over yet another Jurassic movie, with the remote. He's seen these films dozens, if not hundreds, of times, but I know he especially loves to watch them with us. It's as though his enjoyment of the actual movie is enhanced because the people he loves are sharing it with him. Irrelevant that it's neither mine nor your cup of tea. Ben seems to love it more because we're there and I want to give him as many of those special little moments with the time I have left.

❧❧

I wake just as the movie credits are rolling. Looking across at the large round Papasan chair, I smile at Ben who has curled up into a small ball. He's always been the peaceful sleeper. Sometimes, I wake up completely reversed in my bed from where I started, but Ben has always stayed exactly in the same position. Even when he was a baby and you would ask me to watch him for 2 minutes, I just stared at him, because once he's asleep, he's out. I consider waking him gently to send him to bed, but he looks so comfortable that I don't want to disturb him. That must be what you thought about the two of us, as I notice you're missing from the armchair. My neck is stiff from the sofa cushions and I decide to head to my bed. Passing your room, a glow peeks through the not quite closed door. I think I hear you giggle.

"G'night Mom." I call out to you.

"Goodnight Chelsie, I love you." Your voice sounds soft, and I push your bedroom door open a little further. Your face is relaxed as you concentrate on your phone screen in your lap. You catch my eye through the opening door. A look of guilt sweeps across your face fleetingly. If I hadn't been peeping through the crack, I wouldn't have caught the change.

"Are you going to bed? I should go and wake Ben now too. I wanted to wait until the end of the movie." You smile at me. Your phone vibrates and you slip it under the duvet to quieten it. I realize you don't want me to ask who you're texting, and the pink flush of your cheeks tells me all I need. It's been a long time since I've noticed that sort of look on your face.

I take the few strides towards your bed and hug you extra tight. "Goodnight Mom, love you." You squeeze me back. I want to sit on the edge of the bed and ask who you're texting and where did you meet, but I also know you'll feel the need to play down your enthusiasm and excitement. You always feel guilty for being happy and I don't want you to have to dilute your feelings for my benefit, so I say nothing and slide back through the crack in the doorway, heading to my room.

I lay in my bed and draw hearts on my whiteboard. Little perfect love hearts. Cupid hearts with bows through them. Broken hearts with jagged edges. I draw and draw until the board is almost full and resembles my usual scribbles.

Dear Mom, I'm sorry

Chapter 12

The sun streams through the open curtains. It's too bright and harsh for my eyes. Why is it so sunny so early? I wonder. Grabbing my phone off my bedside table, I check the time. It's 11:30, I can't believe I slept in so late. Normally, I wake around 5:30 and watch videos in my room until I hear you or Ben stirring. The TV sound from the living room informs me that Ben is watching cartoons.

I slip my feet into my fluffy gray slippers. My backpack has fallen over and spilled its contents onto the floor. Sluggishly, I put my travel pillow and blanket on the top shelf in my closet. The messy overfilled shelves taunt me to clean them, but my lethargic body tells me today is not the day for a closet clean out. Hanging my bag on the back of the door, I notice an envelope peeking out from the side pocket. My name is scribbled on the front in cursive. I open it carefully as a velvet pouch falls into my lap. A postcard with a picture of Hope the dolphin makes me smile. Turning it over, I read dad's scrawl.

Chelsie, spending the day with you at the aquarium has been the highlight of my year. Your compassion and understanding towards every creature at the sanctuary reminded me how kind and caring you are and I just wanted to tell you how proud I am of the young lady you are becoming. Everyone's destiny is not the same. Those of us who are different can struggle to find our path, but I am certain that you will find yours. All obstacles can be overcome, no matter how insurmountable they might seem. I bought you this little keepsake to remind you of your strength every time you wear it. Love always, Dad.

Picking up the robin blue bag from my lap, I loosen its drawstrings and peer inside. A polished silver dolphin glimmers from within. I lift its delicate chain and after several attempts, clasp it around my wrist. The silver is cool against my skin. I snap a picture and forward it to dad. I don't expect a reply as sometimes his phone sits on his bedside table for days. Technology is not his strong point.

I place the postcard and Tiffany pouch in my vanity drawer. I wonder if my awkwardness stems mostly from dad's genes? This gesture is so typical of him. Thoughtful and meaningful, but also confusing. How does someone almost ignore you for a week but then pull out all the stops at the last minute? I wonder if that's why you left him? It's always too little, too late. I swallow down the lump of disappointment that has formed in my throat and head towards the kitchen.

You don't notice my approach. Enjoying a mug of coffee at the breakfast table, the light streams in through the French doors casting a perfect halo above you. You're relaxed, content. I'm not sure what happened when I was away, but you seem like your younger self.

"I can't believe you let me sleep so late." I approach the island where I spy a basket of freshly baked muffins.

"Good morning, honey. How did you sleep? That trip must have really taken it out of you. I can't remember when, if ever, you've slept so late. I checked in on you 3 times this morning and each time you were completely spark out! I'm so glad to see you getting the rest your body needs. Teens actually need more sleep to help them cope better with their

103

hormones and changing bodies. I was reading an article about it the other day." You grab a glass from the cupboard and pour me some freshly squeezed orange juice from the fridge. Handing me a side plate for a muffin, you place the glass on the table opposite you.

"Fill me in on everything you got up to in Florida." You tap the table, encouraging me to join you. Should I ask you the same? To fill me in on what or who has put that smirk on your face when you glance at your phone? For a second I hesitate, but understand perfectly that you're not ready to share that yet.

You want to hear that I had a good trip with Dad and Melanie. That we hung out together, enjoying family movies. I work hard to paint that picture for you. Describing in detail the little coffee shop around the corner from Dad's. I color in the memory, to include Dad and Melanie, leading you to believe that people watching is like a game to us. I know you would be distraught to discover I spent my days alone while they were at the club. To be honest, I prefer to be on my own at Dad's. It's so much easier. He struggles to talk or interact with me, face to face. It's like staying with strangers, welcoming but awkward.

I pull the neck of my t-shirt to the side to show off my impressive tan lines in response to your questions about the weather. My skin is golden brown. My hair highlighted by the sun, sits in a high messy bun and I look well rested, at ease. You grab my two hands.

"I'm delighted you had a such a great time at your Dad's Chelsie. I worry about you so much when you're not here, but seeing how well you are helps me accept that you're growing up. You probably enjoyed having a break from your old mom." Your tone is joking, but I see genuine relief in your eyes. I'm ok, I had a good vacation. You don't need to feel guilty that you enjoyed your time without me.

I shrug my shoulder with a big smile to confirm your words. Relax, I will my positive thoughts to reach you, hoping to help keep that relaxed look on your face for as long as possible. In that split instant, I accept I also had a break. I had a break from pretending. Dad and Melanie take no genuine interest in me, so I don't have to act as convincing at their house. No need to play my best performance. They want to believe that I love sitting by their pool alone day after day and hanging out at the cafe, people watching. For those weeks while I visit, I don't have to put on so much of a show. As draining as it is for you to worry about me every day, it's just as draining for me to pretend, day in, day out. Like now, I want to ask you so badly, who's put this smile on your face? What's his name? But as soon as I do that, your smile will fade. You'll downplay your interest in this guy and the shadow of worry will return to your face. I don't want you to worry about how I'll react and so I say nothing. I squeeze your hands back tightly. You deserve happiness, Mom.

"Chelsie, you're finally up." Ben interrupts our moment and I pull back my hands, continuing to pick the chocolate chips out of my muffin.

"Hey Ben, what's up dude? Have you tried these muffins? They're so delicious!" Your smile widens as Ben fills me with how he was the chief taste tester. He has already tested 3 just to make sure they were good enough for me. The three of us laugh and for just a millisecond I wonder if this is happiness. Enjoying the people you love smiling, laughing. Is that what true happiness is? I wish I could sense it for a moment, just so I know what it feels like.

Chapter 13

Last night in bed, I realized a crucial part to my plan. Since I've been absent, you've concentrated a little more on your own self-care. Your nails are painted and polished, even your toes. You've given your hair a restyle. Not enough that anybody would notice, but enough so that your lengthy outgrown bangs frame your face perfectly when you dip your head a few degrees to the side.

Your skin is glowing and I think you've lost your sweatpants because your outfits are getting cuter and cuter. Without me present, you used your excess energy and channeled it into yourself. I can see it's paying off. Now I've returned, I need to ensure you have more *time off*. To get accustomed to a life without me.

Dear Mom, I'm sorry

I nestle further into my duvet, contemplating how I can help you understand why I have to go and equally prove to you how better off you'll be. You might grieve now, thinking how different things could be, but that's just it, Mom, they will be different. Without me here, you will have so much time and energy. You won't be drained and fatigued from your full-time self-appointed job, protecting me. A large portion of your time is spent worrying about me. You never take space for yourself. By the time you've helped Ben, checked in with Hannah at university, made dinner, folded laundry, showered or bathed (if you're really lucky), there isn't any time left. There's none left for you. You're barely living, simply existing, like me. If I wasn't here, you would reclaim your life and I intend to spend these last few weeks preparing you. Focus on this new life, Mom. The one you deserve.

Pulling on my Lulus, I search my closet for my favorite gray crop top. The vintage one with a mountain outline and the words Montana written across it, in a large print. I don't even know where it came from, but it's my favorite; it feels like a hug. I wash my face with a cleansing wipe and tie my hair in a high ponytail. Surveying my image in the full-length mirror, I nod. I look intent on a mission.

Bounding down the staircase, I pause for a mere second. How hurt would I be if I hurled myself down the stairs? I wondered. Grabbing the handrail, I shake the idea from my brain. The only outcome worse than what I'm living now would be to be paralyzed in a bed on top of all my other problems.

"You're up and ready early." Your face is camouflaged by the steam from the kettle. You reach for another cup to add with your favorite mug on the countertop.

"Tea?" You suggest with a raised eyebrow and cautious smile, checking in if I'm ok. It's only 8:30am and your worry clock is already ticking. I should have stayed in my room, allowing you to embrace your peaceful morning a little while longer.

"Actually, I'm going for a walk." I decline and grab my water bottle to fill from the fridge door. "I really got into a routine at Dad's and I plan to keep it up now I'm home." Lying to you, I flex my arms, "see, check out these guns." Laughing at my silliness, I'm relieved to have silenced your concern for the moment. I kiss you on the cheek and head out the front door.

Stepping onto the street, I realize I haven't figured out what I might actually do with this time. Heading in the same direction as school, I wonder if Luke is in his yard? I will not deny that walking has been helping me recently. No one watches or worries about me when I'm exercising. It's as if I have an invisible *do not disturb* sign above my head. Other people who cross my path might give a nod or catch my eye as we pass, but with my intent stride and Airpods, no one is expecting any interaction from me.

Even though I'm completing this for you, simply being out and not having to act or worry about how you're interpreting my every word and movement is liberating. In the same way that you've had more opportunities to focus on yourself while I've been gone, being left to my own devices at dad's has forced me to realize how much acting I perform each day, here at home.

Can I admit something? Don't tell anyone else though, ok? Don't let Hannah or Ben ever know this. I'm depleted. The acting and pretending will never end. I can only truly be me when I'm alone and no one is observing. The irony is, I don't enjoy being alone, but it's easier than being with anyone else.

Walking past Luke's yard, I'm a little deflated not to see him bounding along the chain link. I continue towards the school and walk around the track for a while. The surrounding field is vibrant with color. Sunny yellow dandelions have filled the school grounds while I've been in Florida. I find a shaded spot under the cherry blossom tree at the far side of the field and sit with all the weeds I've collected on the way. Laying them in front of me, I organize them by size, just like you taught me all those years ago.

Using my thumbnail, I cut a small slit in every stalk. Threading each flower through the next. I don't stop until I have a matching jewelry set. Necklace, bracelet and earrings.

Within grasp are a few fluffy dandelions. You know the ones you watch floating by in the air. I would chase them as a girl, collecting them for wishes. I pick one and twirl it gently in the wind. Blowing away its fluffiness and seeds. Only its head and stalk remain, all the fuzz and seeds flying in the breeze. Mother Nature's cycle of life, renewed. Even a weed has a purpose. I lay on the grass, forming patterns in the moving clouds.

On my way home, too engrossed with the music, I don't notice Luke approaching the corner. His tail wags uncertainly. Like me, he doesn't understand what happy is. He glances at me sideways, hesitant.

"Hey buddy." I stoop down, kneeling by the bush. Our secret place. His tail now forming loops. He sniffs my fingers as I slip them through the metal holes. He lifts a paw up against my hand.

"High five, good boy." His paw pads are caked in muck and mud. "I missed you. Did you miss me?" Opening my water bottle, I poke its spout through the fence. Tilting it against his lip, he licks greedily as the water trickles into his mouth. We play this drinking game for a few more minutes until he is no longer thirsty and returns to fervently cleaning my fingers. Even though he's unkempt, I allow him to continue. I hope this is not the only human contact he's enjoyed all summer.

"It's not fair, Luke. We're in the wrong lives." I wish I could change places with him, like souls or spirits. I wouldn't mind if his owner ignored me or barely fed me. Luke would love to live in our house and run around the garden with Ben or even snuggle under the covers with you. He would keep your feet warm at night! Ugh, life is backwards.

He whines and lifts his paw to my hand again. I can barely make out his nails, so deeply encrusted. I pour some water onto my bandana and rub it against his paw. It's useless. Years of neglect can't be undone by my damp cloth. Luke licks at the water drops on his paw as I continue my feeble attempts to help break down the caked in mud. We sit there for over an hour. Luke hesitantly offers his paws, one at a time, for me to rub them as much as I can. As the hardened dirt softens and crumbles, I discover the reason for Luke's whining. Some of his nails are so long, they've curled under. Others are splintered, broken off, and one is missing! I kind of wish I hadn't cleaned them now. Before, I simply thought he was dirty, but now I know he's in discomfort. I can't unsee it.

"I'll come back tomorrow, ok Lukeee loo?" He tilts his head in reply to my sing song voice. I want to comfort him, reassure him that he has a friend, he's not alone. Removing my fingers from the holes in the metal netting, I hoist myself back onto my feet. My legs are stiff from sitting for too long. Luke jumps up, bounding along the perimeter until we reach the division with his neighbor's patio. I give him a little wave and promise him I'll be back. He attempts climbing the metal pole in the corner, desperate to escape his imprisoned lot and I feel bad, leaving him behind. I carry on walking, to make it easier for him. No point in dragging out our goodbyes. As I approach the intersection, his bark beckons me to return. I glance over my shoulder. He's running in circles and barking so loud. He wants to join me, but he can't. I mustn't offer him too much kindness. It will only be harder on him in the end.

I jog the rest of the way home, attempting to flee the feeling in the pit of my stomach, from having left Luke behind. The wind whips at my eyes, and a drop escapes my eyelid, sliding down my cheek. Just for a second, I think it's a tear, and I smile. But it's only the wind. It's been years since I've cried. I guess that's one upside to being numb, because I still remember the days when all I ever did was sob. Seems ironic now that I almost miss the act of crying, the pleasure of release.

Chapter 14

I've started to clean out my room. The idea of you having to sift through my things, to figure out what to do with it all is too much to bear. My intent is to purge now, so it will be less for you to go through later. When you look in my closet. You'll see that I've already organized things into different boxes. Some things are for the memory box for Hannah and Ben. Some things for you, for Dad. And the rest can just go to goodwill. You don't need to hold reminders around this house of me. The point of me not being here anymore is not for you to live in memories. To live with ghosts surrounding you. But for you to enjoy the opportunity to be free. Please make sure that you follow through with my instructions for my belongings.

I've been texting Hannah. I'm arranging to go visit her next week. This will allow you to have another few days for yourself. Getting used to having more free time without me around. An opportunity to continue your self-care. Enjoying living in the moment. Not having to filter your feelings or hide your happiness.

Also, I know when I'm gone. Hannah will blame herself. She'll think she should have noticed something, or should have spent more time with me. Mom, don't let her do that to herself. In the same way that you're not to blame. Neither is Hannah nor Ben, and I don't want them thinking there's something they could have done. The whole point of me writing and documenting this journey is to prove there isn't anything anyone can do. I've tried and failed and tried again. It's pointless.

This week, I intend to keep up with my workout façade, and making sure this room is ready for my departure. I hope reading all of this does not make you reflect on these past days too intently. With this new information, looking to lay blame. Wondering if you should have noticed something. Accepting a responsibility which is not yours. Wishing for change. Try to remind yourself that even though all this information is new to you, it's been this way for me my whole life. If there was a way to change, if I was supposed to have found a reason to live, I would have found it by now. Living for other people, living to give other people feelings could never be enough for me. My aim is that you truly understand that. To understand it enough that you could defend it to others, to yourself.

I always thought, or I guess hoped, as I got older, that whatever is wrong with me, would fade. Like I would grow out of it, the same way I did with wetting the bed. But I didn't. I just grew into my headspace even further. Analyzing my thoughts. Watching and learning. Surveying but not taking part.

You know, it's like a movie. I'm some side small character. That doesn't really have a point in the movie, but is always there. That's how I feel. If I feel anything at all. And in days to come when you're struggling. When you're searching for me. When you're looking for reasons. I hope you'll remember this. May these words bring comfort to you. To know that finally I made a decision for myself. Based solely on just my needs. Not on anyone else's emotions. Not considering anyone else's' wishes. Just for me.

117

After my purging. I have filled an entire bag of garbage that I store in the garage. Grabbing my sneakers from the front closet, I lace them up to go for a run. I've raided the bathroom drawers and I've found different files and nail clippers. I'm not sure if any of these will work on Luke's hard and roughened nails, but I'm sure willing to try.

"Just going out for a run," I call out, opening the front door.

"Be safe". You remind me from the kitchen. I gently close the front door on your chirpy voice. It's tone signaling your approval. I'm working out, looking after my best interest. You like that, it reassures you I'm doing well. The more I can convince you I'm fine. The greater distance I can put between us. The more I can prepare you.

Rounding the corner, I can already see Luke's yard, but no sign of him. If he doesn't come out today, I'm not really sure what I'll do with my time. I didn't plan an alternative. Nearing closer, I glimpse his fluffy tail wagging in the overgrown grass.

"Were you hiding from me, Luke?" He rolls over on his back, with his paws excitedly jiggling in the air. I settle down

118

into our spot and encourage him to mimic my hand against the fence with his paw. "Did you miss me? I missed you too." I giggle as he slobbers all over my fingers, poking through the fence. Unzipping my pouch, I pull out what can only be described as industrial sized nail clippers. I don't know who in our home could have ever possible used these, but they look strong and the opening might be just wide enough to slide Luke's nails into. I poke it through the fence and with my other hand try to coax Luke's nail into the clippers' mouth. He resists and hides his snout underneath his paws with a whimper. His piercing blue eyes plead with me to leave his paws alone.

"I know they hurt Luke, but they're gonna get worse if I don't help you." He cocks his head to one side as though he understands my every word. I reach inside my bag for the soft cloth wipes I brought with me in my string back pack. I tease it through the fence and gently rub Luke's nails. He's reluctant, but as the dirt crumbles away, I can see the split edges running through his nails. Eventually, with a lot of petting and cajoling, I clean his paws to the best of my ability. Smoothing the rough broken nail edges with a coarse file, "is that better, Lukey Loo?" He licks my fingers which

I feel is in gratitude, but more likely, he's just appreciating the smell of treats I had been bribing him with.

A crack of thunder fills the air. I look around; the view has become gloomy. Sitting in our little hidden spot, I didn't notice the dark gray clouds rolling in. "I've gotta go Luke, you go inside too, ok?" He cocks his head to one side as if trying to better understand. "Go scratch at the door and your owner will let you in." I gather my bag and sling it over my shoulder. The wind whips up around me. The air feels heavy, I can smell the storm in the air. I need to make it home before the rain. You'll worry if you think I'm out in bad weather.

"I'll come back tomorrow, Lukey Loo, now go inside." I point towards his house, but he follows me along the edge of the chain-link fence. A giant rain drop hits my forehead and slides down the arch of my nose. Luke barks loudly at me. "Yes, I'm going." I reassure him and I sprint off as fast as I can towards home. By the time I hit the porch I'm not sure if my face is more wet from sweat or rain, but I'm relieved to have made it before the real downpour starts.

"There you are, Chelsie. I was getting worried." You open the front door and usher me inside. "Did you not notice the clouds rolling in? Where were you? You've been gone a long time." The questions are endless. They've been rolling around your head while I've been gone and, in your relief, you're firing them at me, one after the other.

Shaking my head, I smile at you and grab two throws from the blanket box in the living room. "How about if we sit on the rocking chairs under the porch like when I was little?" The invitation works like a smile. The frown lines on your forehead smooth and your mind stills as you recollect how I needed to watch storms when I was younger, so I could see them happening. They intrigued me and I loved listening to all the sounds. The thunder crackling against the earth, weak branches falling off the old oak in the front yard, the wind howling at the windows and the rain tap tapping at the glass. The chaos was always comforting to me, like the sky had too many feelings and just needed to let them all out at once. You smile and reach for my hand as I catch you staring at me. "You know how much I love you, Chelsie, right?" Your voice cracks a little at the end. I grab your hand and give it a gentle squeeze.

"I know Mom, I always know. Never think that I don't, ok?" Leaning my head towards you, your eyes soften. I

121

don't let go of your hand and we sit on our rockers with our hands joined in the middle and watch as the angry storm rolls in. In this moment, with the wind whipping around the porch and the raindrops pelting the rosebush by the side gate, I imagine that this is what peace feels like.

Chapter 15

Before my eyes even open, I'm awakened by the endless chirping of the birds outside. Laying snuggled in my cool soft cotton sheets, I keep my eyes closed and try to decipher how many birds I can hear. One is doing a simple *tweet-tweet* every 20 seconds or so. Another hasn't stopped for air and although not very loud, its little *tweet, tweet, tweet* is incessant. Maybe it isn't one, maybe it's a few babies together? Clenching my eyes, I focus intently on the little chirps. Yes, they are overlapping. Their chirps are quiet, weak but they are multiple. Their nest must be close to my window because I can hear them distinctly now. I make a mental note to check out the yard with Ben later.

A shrill cackle followed by an annoying knocking sound announces the arrival of the little red breasted wood pecker that often hangs out in the front yard. Now, I know that any chance of getting back to sleep is lost. I open my eyes. The room is bright with the sun gleaming through the sheer curtains at my window. Last night's dark and gloomy storm quickly erased. The little birds will fly around all day, rebuilding their nests. Finding new treasures in the debris left over from the aftermath of the winds. My closet door is half open, the mess from within taunts me. I have to finish purging. I'll tackle it this afternoon when I pack my bag for my visit with Hannah.

I reach for my phone on the dresser beside me. 'Hey, I'm just wondering if you might be up for a visit this weekend?' I hit the send button on my phone. I know Hannah's schedule is busy teaching summer school, so I don't wait for a reply. Pushing back the bedcovers, I grab my fluffy robe from the back of my door.

The hallway is still dim, and the house is quiet. You and Ben are not up yet. I quietly make myself some cereal and think of casual ways to introduce the idea of me visiting Hannah, without raising any suspicion.

"You're up early, Chelsie. You started some great commitments at your dads. Early mornings, daily workouts,

I'm so proud of you." You lean down to kiss my cheek and the smell of your perfume engulfs me. It's a flowery scent I would recognize anywhere. The smell of home. I smile in reply as you busy yourself making coffee. "What plans have you got for today? Only a few weeks of summer left and it's back to school. Time really is flying by!"

I see my opportunity and grab it. "Actually, I was just thinking the exact same thing. Such a shame that Hannah couldn't come home this summer break. I was hoping I could visit her for a bit. Do you think she would like that?" I hate manipulating you this way, but I know by asking your advice you'll feel involved and positive. You'll support this whim.

"What a great idea. Wow, my two girls, so grown up. I wish I could get the time off work and join you, but sadly, no rest for the wicked." Your tone is fun and whimsical. My task accomplished.

Ben shuffles his feet across the floor, slouching into the chair opposite me at the bistro table. His eyes squint against the sunlight streaming through the French doors. His hair is disheveled. Each strand in a different direction to its neighbor.

"Looks like you've had quite a night, Ben." I tease him jokingly.

"I made a fort in my room and slept in it. I guess I didn't construct it too well because when I woke up it had fallen in and I was wrapped up in the *roof* blanket." He explains, without a hint of amusement. I stare back at him until I see the left corner of his mouth twitch. I glance across the kitchen and catch your eye. The two of us burst out laughing and after a moment's hesitation, Ben joins in. This is what I think happiness might feel like. The sun highlighting our smiles and the birds chirping in the background of our laughter. For this moment, our little world is at peace.

Returning to my room, I check my phone. There's a message notification from Hannah. 'I'm super busy, but if you just want a place to chill without mom hovering over you, I've got you! I'm free most evenings, but in the day, I have classes so you'll need to keep yourself busy, ok?'

I already knew Hannah was teaching classes over the summer. You were so proud when you announced to Ben and me how she wouldn't be coming home because she had been offered a position to assist with summer school. I owe

Hannah a proper visit, a real goodbye. I text her back 'Packing and booking train ticks now. See you on Thursday x.'

Returning to the kitchen, I mention texting with Hannah and how she's so excited that I'm coming to visit. The slight tightening of your lips betrays the concern you attempt to cover with your happy tone.

"That's great honey." For a split second you hesitate, your mouth pauses open, ready with some of your rapid-fire questions. Your brow relaxes into place and your mouth slowly closes. Whatever it is you wanted to caution, to advise, to counsel, you've thought better of it. Instead, you smile and pat my hand.

'I guess you really are all grown up, Chels. You don't need me organizing you anymore.' I can tell you're a teeny-weeny bit sad, but I also know the distance I am placing between us is necessary.

"Hey Ben, a lot of chirping woke me this morning. Shall we check out the backyard and see if we can spot any nests?"

Ben's eyes widen. "Do you think it's the same little robin as last year?" He muffles through the mouthfuls of cereal he is shoveling into his mouth in a rush to explore the yard.

"Slow down," I urge him. We'll check as soon as we're both dressed. He nods and I return to my room to get ready.

Within minutes, Ben is tapping at my door. "Chels, I'm ready, let's go." He has neither washed his face nor brushed his hair, but at least he's slipped on a Pokémon t-shirt to wear with his pajama shorts. I giggle at his eagerness.

We spend an hour scouring the yard and find a small nest in the shrubs underneath my window. "She looks exactly the same as Scarlett. Do you think she could know to come back to the same place as last year?" Ben is busy zooming in on his phone camera and taking shots of the red-breasted bird and her chicks. "Why are their eyes still closed?" Ben wonders and I quickly google his question.

"Ohh these chicks must be brand new. Their eyes can stay closed until day 5." I inform him. "Their feathers will grow from day 3." I read out the key points I feel will interest Ben.

"I'm going to compare these pictures with the ones we took last year, to see if this new bird really is Scarlett." Ben whispers, eager not to scare the mother bird with her chicks. "Shall I dig up some beetles and worms to help the mother out?" Ben wonders.

I assist him to find a suitable container and place it in the shade with some cool earth. He lifts one of the stone path pavers. "Bingo, look at all the treasure I've found Chelsie." He beckons me over. I watch as the exposed worms try to wiggle their way back into the earth but they aren't fast enough. Ben uses his long bug tweezers to pick them up, placing them in the container.

"I'm out now Ben. Birds I'm fine with, but bugs are too much for me." Ben laughs as he continues to catch the squirming bugs. "I'm heading back inside but you stay here and watch mama bird. Don't go too close and don't leave out too many worms for her, ok? She still needs to forage for her own family." He is keen to help, but I want him to learn how instinctively our little friend will know how to look after her offspring. I ruffle his hair and head back inside.

୭∽ଡ଼

Later, when I'm sorting through more of my mess in the closet, I hear you giggling in your room. I can't make out the full conversation, but I know for sure you are not talking to aunt Regina. Your voice is light and feminine. Laughing and

129

teasing. I quietly creep into the hallway to better hear what you're saying, but my shadow across the landing light must have spooked you. I only hear the end of your call.

"Yes, ok. I'll see you Sunday, now go." The faint creak of your bed springs informs me you're getting up. I run back to my room in stealth mode. Seconds later, you push my open door a little further. "Still cleaning? You really are committing to this new lifestyle." Laughing, you lean down to hug me goodnight. The flush on your cheeks is one I haven't seen in years and in that split second, I know the time is coming closer. You're almost ready. I squeeze you back extra tight. We don't hug much anymore. What if this is the last hug I give you? I try to put all my love into it. You lean back slightly and look into my eyes. "You sure you're ok Chels?" Your syrupy tone is gone, replaced with concern.

"Yep, just want you to know how much I love you, Mom." Your eyes well and you nestle back into our embrace. Now you squeeze me extra tight and I pray to God (even if I'm not sure if he really exists) that this memory, these hugs will help keep you warm.

Chapter 16

Did you know trains and planes are my favorite way to travel? Anywhere with crowds, really. It's so easy to disappear, to vanish amongst all the different cultures, languages and personalities. An older lady is talking loudly to her son, informing him that the train is running 7 minutes late so far. She'll keep him (and the rest of us in her carriage) informed of any changes. A tall lanky boy is watching noisy videos on his phone, oblivious to the death stares from the surrounding passengers. No one will look or question me the entire journey. I won't need to second guess my actions, my facial expressions, nothing. I can just be.

Popping in my Airpods, I watch Tiktoks for most of the journey until I receive a notification that I have a new email from James. Shoot, he's going to be in town next week.

He wants to meet. I was kind of hoping to send him an email before schools back, saying how busy life is getting and not to worry if he doesn't hear from me. Hoping he'll assume I'm just living my best life, too busy to respond to him. His emails would dwindle and eventually he would assume I ghosted him. Now I'm going to have to figure out another plan.

I hit the reply button. 'Hey James, that's great news. My schedule is a little busy, so text me when you're free. I hope we can meet up. Talk soon, Chelsie.' I hit send and hope my vagueness deters his enthusiasm to meet up. Closing my email, I open my music app. I hit play and allow the music to soothe me. Leaning my head against the train window, the world outside swooshes by. Closing my eyes, I imagine scribbling on my erasable pad. Denting the pad so hard until my mind stops whirring, stops worrying. Scribbling to the sound of the thump-thump of the train on its tracks.

I wake to the general hustle and bustle of people getting out of their seats and reaching for their bags. Wiping the side of my mouth and corners of my eyes just to make sure I don't have any crusties.

'Train has arrived. I'll grab an Uber and see you soooooooon.' I hit send to Hannah and follow the rest of the carriage off the train to the taxi ranks outside the station.

Within minutes, I'm settled into an Uber and on my way. The vibration of my phone announces an incoming message. 'I'm still finishing today's classes, but my friend Isaac is there and he'll let you in. Can't wait to see you! I'll be home by 4, ok?' I reply with a heart emoji. I hadn't thought about Hannah working. Luckily, her friend can stay and let me in or I would have been walking around Charlotte for the afternoon.

Pulling up outside the apartment and I can see why Hanna loves it here so much. The complex is called the Edge and though I had seen pictures of it, they did not do it justice.

I walk through the large steel entrance beside the gate and take in the view. Breathtaking, similar to a five-star resort. There's a community building to the right, which houses a convenience store and a pizzeria. Beside that, there is a walk-in pool that is surrounded by cabanas. Hot tubs are nestled amongst palm trees on the opposite side of the pool and there's even a dining area. I'm doubtful any student could get any work done here. How is Hannah even affording this? I thought students lived in dingy, windowless basement rooms. I walk towards the closest building of apartments in search of her place.

By the time I arrive at the door, beads of sweat are dripping down the back of my neck. It's so hot today, maybe I could wait for Hannah down by the pool? Right, but I still need to change and leave my bag at her place. Finally, I knock half-heartedly on the door, secretly hoping no one will answer. My hopes are dashed. The door swings open and a blond boy with floppy hair greets me.

"You must be Chelsie. Come in, come in." He moves his body to the side and ushers me in with the flourish of his arm. "I'm Isaac, so nice to finally meet you." His friendly face is genuine. My earlier hesitation subsides.

"Thanks so much, I'm Chelsie." The heat rises to my cheeks, embarrassed, unsure of what to say exactly.

"I know that silly." Isaac swats at me playfully.

"I feel like I already know everything about you." He's grinning at me excitedly and I sense that he'll be disappointed if I admit I've never even heard his name before today, so I smile, nodding my head in agreement.

"When Hans told me yesterday you were coming, I insisted on being here to welcome you. Not gonna lie, the Edge can seem a little daunting when you first arrive, but luckily, it's summer break, so we have the place to ourselves." He continues his welcome monologue all the while, opening cupboards, pouring juice and grabbing a fruit tray from the fridge. He sets it all out on the coffee table before me.

"Sorry, I wasn't sure what you liked, so I made a little selection." He watches me keenly as I take some pieces of watermelon and kiwi. I pop a slice into my mouth and smile my appreciation. He claps his hands delightedly and leans further back in the wicker egg chair opposite me. How can Hannah afford this place? It's how I imagine an apartment on Fifth Avenue would be. There are floor to ceiling glass doors that lead to a huge balcony overlooking the pool area.

"So, what do you feel up to? Swimming or napping?" The enthusiasm shining from his twinkling gray eyes encourages me to admit that I wouldn't mind a dip in the pool.

"Awesome. Let me put your bag in Han's room so you can get yourself ready and we will head down to the pool. I'll pack us a cooler." He opens a door to the left of the kitchen, which leads to a beautiful bedroom. It's almost nicer than yours, Mom. A huge king bed with a tufted linen headboard takes center stage. A wall filled with sliding barn doors is on the other side. I slide one, to peek in Hannah's closet. In the center, there is a small walkway leading to the most luxurious ensuite I've ever seen. Are we rich and no one told me? This place is better than our home! No wonder Hannah wanted to stay here all summer. Who wouldn't?

I walk away from the jacuzzi tub and back to the bed to unpack my bikini from my bag. I change quickly. Grabbing a tube of sunscreen, a hat, and my phone, I return to the kitchen.

"I can't believe how fancy this place is." I tell Isaac as I rejoin him in the open living space.

"Yeah, there's a two year wait list to even get a viewing appointment here. I'm only in because Sven already had this place when I met him. Sven's my main squeeze, you'll meet him later. C'mon, I'll fill you in on all the tea poolside." His voice trails off into a little laugh and I follow him through the complex, enchanted.

For the rest of the afternoon, Isaac talks incessantly, filling me in on the Charlotte social scene and more importantly, his role within it. I am bemused that this quirky, confident boy seems to be Hannah's bestie. At home, in high school, I always thought the friends she brought home were more the nerdy type. They matched Hannah's serious, studious personality. I could never have imagined this unlikely friendship. Isaac seems very familiar, even calling her Han's. I can't imagine calling her Han's, can you?

He continues to talk at me, a mile a minute. I smile and close my eyes. This is easy. This boy needs nor wants any input from me. I can just sit here and be part of it all without contributing, and for just a second, I let go. Relax.

∂∽∾

A shadow crosses my face. I'm still mid slumber. My eyes are closed. My face enjoys the respite from the pelting sun. Stretching my neck and arms, I slowly peel open my eyes. Hannah has arrived and is gesticulating to Isaac. Talking in hushed tones. I love to watch her, she's so entertaining. You know how, with twins, often one is petite, and the other is the tallest in the class? Like as if one atom split? One gets this and therefore the other gets that. This is exactly how

I feel about Hannah and I. She is beautiful and opinionated. An emotional whirlwind. It's like she has everything that I don't. Don't get me wrong, I'm not begrudging to her. I'm not jealous. She's like a sitcom of who I could have been, if I wasn't me, if I wasn't broken.

"Sleeping beauty, you're awake." She's catches me watching her, smiling as she skips towards me. That's the perfect description of Hannah, isn't it? She skips through life. I sit up, just in time for her to launch her entire body onto my lap.

"I missed you so much! I'm so excited you're here." She nuzzles into my neck. I giggle because she expects it. It doesn't tickle anymore or make me laugh, but I think Hannah would be sad if she knew that, so I always still pretend to enjoy it. The look of satisfaction on her face as she pulls away is worth t it. Hannah's smile is like the sun, it brightens everything around it.

"I was just filling Isaac in on my day. Ugh, summer school is the pits." She laughs. Typical Hannah, selected amongst her peers to teach summer school, but she thinks it's worse for her than the students actually attending. She is so focused on her own little path. Not that she thinks she's better than anyone, but like she just doesn't even think about other people. She doesn't appear selfish though, more like quirky. I don't know how she does it. Things just come easy to Hannah.

Heading back to her apartment, we make plans to meet Isaac and Sven for drinks at the tiki bar after we grab some food.

I feel almost grown up being here. It's giving me the smallest glimpse of what it would be like for me, except the opposite. I wouldn't be the social butterfly, because I could never be Hannah and Chelsie is already dead, even if it's just on the inside.

Dear Mom, I'm sorry

Chapter 17

The week has flown by. I must admit, it surprised me when I heard Hannah had a summer job. She's always said summer is her favorite season. She likes to be free to enjoy it.

Every afternoon she comes home and spends another hour or two going through the students' work. Preparing for the following day. I guess she's also growing up, becoming mature and responsible. I always thought Hannah was like aunt Regina, but now I see she's becoming more like you. Teaching others by her own successful example. You can be proud of Hannah.

I've spent the last few days by the pool and the evenings at the tiki bar with Hannah, Isaac, Sven and some of their other student friends. We joined in a quiz night on

Sunday and yesterday we sang karaoke until we cleared out the bar. Isaac and Sven sang I got you babe and I think I hurt my stomach muscles from laughing so much. They're both really fun and nice guys. Hannah is lucky to have such good friends.

I was supposed to be going home today but there's a back-to-school party on Friday and Hannah convinced me to stay the extra few days. She doesn't know that I have things to finish, people to say goodbye to.

Last night she kept reminding me how I have no obligations or plans, so I needed to attend this party. Drunkenly yelling across the room, "You only live once Chels, enjoy it." I've spent my entire life with Hannah. Apart from you, I don't think anyone knows me as well as she does and still, we're worlds apart. She's excited about the party. It's Mamma Mia themed and the boys are dressing up as Meryl Streep. Yep, both of them! Hannah cannot contemplate the idea that I wouldn't be as excited as she is to share this experience. Of course, if I told her this wasn't in my comfort zone, she would apologize at once. Explaining how she forgets to reign in her enthusiasm. Then she might question me. Have I been taking my pills every day? Have I been feeling all right? For a moment she would engage in big sister mode. She'd steal sideways worried glances at me. Concern and pity would flood her face. Yeah, no thanks. It's easier to stay the extra few days. Go to the party and watch Hannah be happy. Watch her enjoying having me here. Showing off her little sister, who's fun and normal, not some unfeeling freak ruining everyone else's good time. For just a few more days, I'll be a normal version of myself. Hannah's version of me.

Dear Mom, I'm sorry

Chapter 18

The party is crazy, or perhaps it isn't. Maybe I am sheltered and unaware. I'm not sure, but either way it is wild.

Firstly, no one warned me that the bathrooms are literally people lining up to snort lines. Like out in the open! Right there as you walk past the stalls. Don't worry, I will not take any drugs or hang out with anyone else doing drugs, well except maybe Isaac and Sven. I didn't see them actually take anything, but they are both in full Meryl mode and singing, slipping through my fingers at any passers-by. The bar area is packed, but every new guest delights in Sven and Isaac's antics, encouraging them further.

Hannah spends most of her night, screeching excitement at seeing friends who have now returned to campus for the new semester. Although many guys try to flirt with her, she seems uninterested. Younger Hannah would have teased them, enjoying the attention. She has grown so much in this last year.

A few guys even flirt with me. They keep asking me what classes I'm enrolled in and not thinking I reply 'all of them', which they think is funny and so I keep up the pretense of being a student myself. A freckled-faced boy by the name of Bradley follows me wherever I go. I spend most of the evening with him. His brown hair falls into perfect curls. His face is not clean shaven, more like a designer stubble. He looks like he put zero effort into getting ready, but I suspect it actually takes him a lot of time to look so perfectly thrown together. He is pretty entertaining with his stories and funny jokes. He likes to weave a story and hold an audience. He is very comfortable for me to be around. I can float into the background. We dance together most of the night. I participate in Beer Pong and even try Limbo. I'm not good at either, but at least I tried.

By the end of the evening, Brad and I are hanging out on a couple of loungers down by the pool area. He traces my cheekbone with his finger and kisses me softly. His stubble feels tickly against my skin. "What do you say we get out of here?" His husky voice whispers in my year as he gently kisses my neck. It's already midnight and I am sure Hannah will not allow me to go elsewhere.

I glance over my shoulder towards the bar. "I think my sister will be ready to leave soon, and I have to stay with her."

He pulls his face into a grimace. "We're all adults. How about if we sneak off to my place?" His fingers gently trace my arm. I feel hesitant. I came here to expose myself to life experiences, but I don't want to cause Hannah worry or concern.

"Chelsie, we've made an executive decision." Isaac's voice calls out to me as he weaves his way down the path towards us.

I roll my eyes at Brad as though I'm annoyed at the intrusion, but secretly I'm glad to have been saved from having to make any rash decisions.

"Chels, are you even listening to me?" Isaac plops onto the lounger beside me.

"What's happening Meryl?" I sit up and face him. He's smoothing out his white skirt.

"Han's, Sven and myself have had an amazing idea! We are taking you to the Myrtle beach festival. How fun is that?" He places his hand on my shoulder. I shake my head and roll my eyes at him. "Don't be a party-pooper, we've already decided. C'mon I have to bring you back with me. We're ready to leave now." He stands up unsteadily and offers his hand to me. I grab it and allow him to help me up. I shrug my shoulders and wave goodbye to Brad, allowing myself to be dragged back to the safety of the Tiki Bar. In all honesty, I was a little out of my depth and I am relieved we are making our way home.

Chapter 19

My first morning at Hannah's, I realized I had forgotten my pills at home. Admittedly, I should have texted you and asked if Dr. Ramsay's office could send a prescription to the local drugstore here in Charlotte, but then I thought, If I'm leaving anyway, do I even need them anymore? I remember how dark and bleak the world is without them, but I'm not planning on being around long enough to let those feelings get a hold of me. I want to *feel* a little something before I go. Even if it is fear and despair. I know I've promised you I would never go off my meds without consulting and speaking to you about alternative options. I understand how disappointed you'll feel reading this.

Anyway, all of that may explain why this morning I woke feeling a little jittery. My hands have a light shake to them and the rhythm of my heart seems set to the beat of rave music. It's different from my usual flatness. I hang around the apartment for an hour, drinking infused tea and watching videos on my phone. Isaac has offered to take me thrifting today to find a perfect outfit for tomorrow's day out. A group of us are heading to Myrtle beach and I wanted to get something cute to wear to the party. Even though I look young, all of Hannah's friends have been so nice, incorporating me into their group. It's almost like having friends. Ok, they're not actually mine, but just for a moment to pretend I'm part of it all. A group, a collective of people with something in common, even if that something is partying.

Isaac and I spend the afternoon in and out of thrift shops. I finally settle on an ancient pair of white Levi's, he's convinced me he will turn into the hottest shorts I've ever seen. To pair it up, I found a bright orange men's Hawaiian style shirt I will wear as a crop top, knotted in the front. When we get back to the complex, Isaac encourages me to go hang by the pool while he works his magic on the Levi's. I'm skeptical to be honest, but I had a nice day out, and the shorts were only $5. Nothing ventured, nothing gained, as you would say!

I return to the apartment after a quick swim to find Hannah hunched over the small desk in the corner of the living room. "Hey, I didn't realize you were back already. I was just down by the pool."

I slide the balcony door to hang my towel out on the railing. Hannah gathers her notes into one pile. "I'm trying to get these assignments completed so I can enjoy Myrtle beach too." She laughs. There are at least three different textbooks open on the desk.

"Do you actually verify their facts, like from each different book?" This seems like a huge amount of work to me, but I am not an academic, so have no idea if that's what people expect at university level.

Hannah shoves her notes into the top drawer and closes the text books, piling them on the corner of her desk. "I like to cross reference their quotes and make sure that they aren't paraphrasing." She laughs affably. "I think that's enough. I can do some more on the drive down or way back." I nod my agreement to her even though we both understand she has no intention of doing either. From what I've gathered over the last few days, Hannah is a real socialite. Everyone in the complex greets her with a friendly wave and a funny reference to their last night out. Of course, Hannah would be the *IT* girl, why wouldn't she? She has it all.

Isaac announces his arrival with a soft tap-tap-tap on the door and enters the center of the room, doing his model sashay finishing with a little twirl in front of the love seat.

"Mademoiselles, I present to you this season's must have; shorts by Zac. My latest creation." He dips into a small curtsy, rolling his arm in a flourish as he stands to full height, in a 'ta-da' moment.

I burst out laughing and quickly explain to Hannah that the ripped, shredded shorts that Isaac is modeling are actually the jeans I bought earlier today. "Those are amazing. How in the world did you make them so trendy?" I was doubtful they were the same jeans. They looked like they came from a high-end fashion designer and not the bargain bin at goodwill!

"I love them. You shall go to the ball, Chelsie," Hannah taps me on the head with the handle end of the broom, like a fairy godmother. Isaac slips the shorts off, to reveal his bright red speedos. I catch Hannah's eye and a new round of giggles set in.

Dear Mom, I'm sorry

Chapter 20

I've never been to Myrtle Beach, as most of our vacations were taken in Florida growing up. The weather in South Carolina is too much of a gamble in early spring dad used to say. Clearly that's not the case mid-august and I feel a small flutter of excitement as Sven navigates his racing green Mini Cooper through the bustling main streets. We pull up to the Merlin Apartments where we've rented a place for the weekend and gratefully climb out of the car to stretch out our legs. The mini is cute, but it was cramped with all 4 of us and our bags. The humidity outside is overwhelming and beads of sweat form at the nape of my neck. I am already missing the ice-cold air conditioning of the mini.

"This way bitches." Hannah hollers back towards us as she heads towards the registration entrance. I pick up mine and Hannah's bags. Sven picks up his and Isaacs's bag with a shake of his head. He hurries to catch up with Isaac who has already skipped ahead to join Hannah. A small laugh escapes my throat and I realize I feel something. A bit of anticipation, mixed with excitement and maybe some nerves? I'm not sure exactly, but something! Omg, what if I'm cured? What if I'm better and all this time it's just been my rotten meds making me detached? I can feel the adrenaline coursing through my veins. I catch up with the others as they are being issued keys. "There you are Chels, come, let's check this place out." She skips up the concrete steps to the second floor and leads us down the walkway to room 212. The cold air hits us upon entering and we collectively breathe a sigh of relief.

"Wow, that's some heatwave out there." Isaac mops his brow with a piece of kitchen towel.

Sven pops his head out from a doorway, "Come check out the rainfall shower, I'm sure we can figure a way to cool you off!" Isaac runs towards the room and I venture down the small hallway to find Hannah, leaving the echoes of what sounds like a pillow fight, behind me.

I find Hannah in a beachy themed room at the end of the hallway. The headboard is made from reclaimed driftwood and the bedspread is decorated with shells. There's even a glass door leading to a balcony with a rattan swing chair. I feel the smallest twinge of jealousy, wishing I had found this room first. Having not financially contributed, I know I'll have to settle for the pullout couch in the living room. "This room will be perfect for you Chels, what do you think?" Hannah's lips curl into a smile and I can't tell if she's teasing or for real. She walks back down the hallway to another door and opens it with a flourish. "Check it out sis, this is the pièce de résistance!" She jumps on the oversized king bed as I ooh and aah over the sunken jacuzzi in her ensuite and the double bed swing lounger on the balcony.

"How do you guys even afford this?" I laugh giddily. It's like we've won the lottery and I am fast becoming accustomed to this beach vibe lifestyle.

"Girls, meeting in the kitchen, please." Isaac's voice is faint. I look towards Hannah. She bounces off her bed, skipping to the kitchen.

Sven is pouring the last shot of tequila and has the salt and lime at the ready. "Lick, shoot, suck!" He lifts his glass to us and we all follow suit. The lime is bitter, but I bite down harder, hoping it will distract me from the sharpness of the tequila. "Let's get into our 'kinis and check out the pool scene. What do you guys think?" Sven asks, but he's already pouring more shots.

"That sounds great. I'll go get changed." I announce, edging towards the hallway and far away from the new shots being poured. Alcohol is a natural depressant and I must be careful not to overindulge.

I hear them taunting, come back 'lightweight' and smile as Hannah reminds them that I'm only 16. She's such a great big sister, always happy to include me but also protecting me at all costs. Unpacking my small bag, I pull out my neon green bikini. I once read an article in a magazine that said to wear fluorescent colors at outdoor events for others to find you easily. I'm hoping that advice works tonight. If I'm to be 100% honest, I'm kind of hoping Brad might make an appearance later. Isaac mentioned him enquiring if I was coming on this trip, so I'm hoping that's a good sign. Nothing happened between us the other night, but tonight might be different.

Isaac and Sven make cocktails with the blender they found in the kitchen while Hannah and I get ready. I don't know how he did it, but these shorts look fire. Teamed with a ribbed white crop top and the Hawaiian shirt in a front tie, my outfit is perfect. I've curled the ends of my hair but just a little, each tendril falling into a soft curl as though it has a wave to it. A little gloss and mascara complete my look. It's too hot outside to wear any real make up. The little thump, thump in my heart is there again. I feel excited.

We walk down to the beach just after 9 and it is packed. I don't know what I was expecting, like some camp chairs around an open fire, but this is another level. There are beer tents and food trucks set out along the edge of the beach. Speakers and lights surround the DJ on his makeshift stage from old pallets. Girls in grass skirts are taking in the event money while placing a lei around each guest's neck. They give me a white and orange one that compliments my outfit perfectly. Sven and Isaac received bright green and yellow lei's and are none too impressed. "Why couldn't I have a red one to match the flowers on my shirt?" Isaac may have had tasted too many cocktails in the kitchen. He makes a move to return to the greeters, but Sven swiftly catches his elbow as he stumbles backwards and leads him to a beach chair.

"I thought it was you." Too busy watching Sven and Isaac, I turn to find Brad facing me. He is wearing light blue golf shorts with a coordinating shirt which is also front tied like mine and 90% of the other females here. I laugh out loud. "Don't be a judger," he warns. "Equality for everyone. I'm hot too." He laughs easily and I take in just how hot he is. His shirt is pulled taut against his firm chest and his perfectly smooth skin is glistening, from what I suspect is baby oil and not sweat, like myself. He steps closer to me, his nose only inches from mine. He bends his head so slightly. "I like your hair curled like this." His voice is barely a whisper and I move forward just a teeny bit to hear him better. He twirls one of my curls on his fingers and drops it as his hand caresses my arm until he entwines his fingers with mine. "I've been waiting for you." He smiles and gives my fingers a little squeeze. In that moment, I know I will succumb to whatever this man asks. In that split second, I suddenly understand the meaning of desire.

"Hey Brad, maybe remind yourself she's only 16." Hannah returns from the drinks tent and passes me a bottle of water with a raised eyebrow.

"I was going to get you a Margarita, but then I saw you over here and figured it might be time for you to mix in a water. You too Brad, maybe you need a water, eh?" Hannah's tone is playful but her words hit their mark as Brad disentangles his fingers from mine. He rolls his eyes and mouths 'see you later' as he slinks past Hannah towards the refreshment tent. I feel like I should be mad, but I felt totally out of my depth and a teensy bit of me is grateful that Hannah interrupted the moment. She stares me down intently. "Chels, what do you think you were doing? Brad is a player, be careful, ok?"

"I just wanted to play a bit, too." The words are out of my mouth before I can check myself and I hold my breath, watching as shock overtakes Hannah's features. Her sharp intake of breath forewarns me of the lecture I am about to receive but as if the wind suddenly changed, she bursts out laughing. She's literally doubled over, holding onto her sides like she might fall apart. I'm relieved to have avoided the lecture, but I'm seriously wondering if she's not having some sort of seizure. "Oh my, Chelsie, you never cease to amaze me. You really are growing up and I need to stop over protecting you but Brad is on another level ok? He's not the playmate for you!" With a flashback to Brad's well-oiled chest, I too join in her ridiculous laughter.

"Like honestly, what would I even do with a guy like Brad?" The question is rhetorical but Hannah is keen to reply.

"I'm sure you could think of many things to do with him and if not, he would certainly have had some ideas! Luckily, I swooped in to save you before things went too far." She reassures me, taking my hand, leading me to the dance floor. As we dance the night away, I wonder if *too far* is exactly where I was hoping Brad would take me.

Chapter 21

I didn't sleep well, barely at all, if I'm honest. The beach party was fun, and I loved dancing under the stars with Hannah. I hope it will be one of her favorite memories. This week we've had together has been special and I know when I'm gone, she'll look back on these days with a smile.

Brad never returned to find me last night. Barely an hour after Hannah had scolded him, I saw him leading a tall red head towards the waters' edge, into the shadows. He was smiling at her in the exact same way he had at me. How could I have been so silly to think he had been interested in me? Feelings or not, I will never understand men. He replaced me so quickly, so easily, like I was nothing. I tossed and turned most of the night, trying to think how I could have behaved differently, more interesting, made a more lasting impression on him.

The past few days, I have secretly been hoping that I'm fixed. Without my medication, so many emotions have come back to me. Excitement, hope, anticipation, it's been great, but there are no ups without downs and I felt every single negative emotion throughout the night. I'm feeling dejected and exhausted now. I just want to go home. Back to the safety of our house, with people who understand me. The onslaught of anxiety and worthlessness that hounded me through the night, has quickly erased the few good feelings I've had this week. The thump, thump of excitement that lasts mere moments could never outshine the dark and gloom that intend to be my companions today.

I hear the others singing and laughing as they're making coffee in the kitchen. I burrow a little further under the bedspread and let out a muffled scream. Yesterday I would have joined them and maybe even grabbed the bottle of orange juice as a mic and danced around the living room, but that girl is gone. The real me is here now. They probably didn't even want me to join them on this trip. They've most likely been putting up with me because I'm Hannah's little sister. Isaac probably only took me shopping because he felt sorry for me. Perhaps Hannah asked him to, so she wouldn't have to spend so much time with me? My thoughts are spiraling out of control. I close my eyes and pretend I'm scribbling away each and every emotion. Slowing my breathing down, I breathe in for a count of five and release slowly, as slow as I can. Willing my heart beat to relax, my mind to calm down. I shake the obtrusive thoughts away. I need to focus on something productive.

I untangle myself from the knot of covers that I've balled into and sit on the edge of the bed. My clothes are strewn across the floor. Slowly collecting each item, I add them to my travel bag. I quietly open the bedroom door and sneak into the bathroom across the hall. I glimpse myself in the mirror. My hair looks matted and wild. Tear tracks have left paths of destruction through last night's make-up. Smudged mascara accentuates the dark circles under my eyes. I hold on to the side of the sink as I peer closely at myself. *Come back Chelsie*, I urge to the sad-looking girl in the mirror, but she can't hear me. I stare deep into her eyes, knowing it's futile. She's looking right through me, like I'm no longer here.

༄༅

Hannah pops her head into my room as I'm packing my last bits and pieces. "You ok Chels?" Her voice is soft and concerned. She also saw Brad slink off with his red head at the party.

"I'm all ready." I turn towards her, "just feeling a little rough today." I crinkle my nose with a half-hearted smile, hoping she'll leave me alone.

She holds her hands up, facing me. "Gotcha, I'll inform the boys you're experiencing your first hangover and we'll go easy on you. You can sleep all the way back to Charlotte." She's already down the hall on her way to inform Sven and Isaac of my delicate condition. Perfect, I'll let them all think that I'm a terrible drinker who has a chronic headache today. Just one more reason they'll be glad when I've left tomorrow! I'm ready to leave. I'm ready to say goodbye. I know my days are limited. My feelings might have returned, but they are simply one more example of how broken I truly am.

Chapter 22

The train ride is never ending. I found a quiet spot at the back of the third carriage and hoped to sleep the entire way home, but my rambling thoughts have decided otherwise. Even writing in my journal is not helping. I struggle to hold the pen with my shaking fingers.

I'm overwhelmed with feelings and emotions. I knew stopping my meds would mean darkness and anxiety would set in, but I don't think I expected to feel so much so soon. I can barely scramble my thoughts together. My whole body is jittery.

Hannah popped into my room this morning to say goodbye. She leaned down to hug me and a tear escaped from the corner of my eye. "Wow, I can't remember the last time I've seen you cry Chels. I'm glad you've had such a great week with us, and I can't wait for you to come back." She gently wiped the tear stain from my cheek and rubbed my arm reassuringly. I nodded my reply, scared my hoarse throat would betray me. "I'll Facetime mom on Friday for Ben's birthday. Be careful getting home and never forget how much I love you, ok?" I swallowed back my emotions and squinted, smiling at her through my tears. As the door softly closed, I longed to run after her and tell her everything I needed to say, but I couldn't.

Goodbye Hannah. The tears well and fall in large droplets through my damp lashes.

Thanks for being the best big sister anyone could ever hope for. Thanks for letting me learn from you. Allowing me to watch and mimic you all these years so my life could be as close to normal as it could be for a person like me.

Thanks for being my first friend even if you ended up being my only one for all these years. I didn't need anyone else anyway. You understood me completely. When I couldn't put feelings into words, you knew. You taught me so much by allowing me to shadow you all these years and for that I am so truly grateful.

Thanks for showing me how to use a tampon when I was 13. For gluing the doves' head back on the porcelain ornament in the front room. The one I broke when I was 11 (Sorry Mom!). Most of all, thanks for voicing my feelings throughout the years, when I could not.

Pulling my sweater closer to my face, I hide my tears. I close my eyes and concentrate only on the thud thudding of the train as it races home along the track.

⮞⮜

I don't know if I actually slept or was just dazed for the rest of the journey, but the next time I open my eyes, we have arrived at the station. I grab my bag and descend onto the platform, working my way past the other travelers. I order an Uber from the app on my phone and head outside to wait for the black dodge journey that has been assigned to me.

My heart feels heavy, as though it's weighing down my entire being. Every step is an effort. I feel as though I can't breathe. I take a deep breath and hold it to a count of 5 before slowly releasing it to a count of 10, just like you taught me when I was little. Sadly, just like then, it isn't working now either. I practice some more, willing myself to calm down. My knee is ever so slightly shaking, it feels as though it might give way. My legs may buckle beneath me and I'll just lie here on the floor, in a puddle.

The black Dodge pulls up in front of me and the passenger window rolls down.

"Chelsie?" The bearded driver asks? I nod and open the back door. I push my bag forward and slide onto the cool leather seats. Quiet jazz music is playing and though I can't stand this style of music, I lean my head against the window with my eyes shut as though enjoying it. I don't want to give the driver any opportunity to talk. I'm not interested in filling some stranger in on my trip. I keep my eyes clenched the entire ride home as I urge my pulse to calm down. Before you see me in this state, I need to get a hold of myself. How am I going to explain my stained, streaked face? My sunken eye sockets, their dark rings highlighting every missed minute of sleep. How will I hold myself together over the next few days until I say goodbye?

Exiting the vehicle, I notice your car is missing from the driveway and I am so grateful to the gods (or whoever) for this small reprieve. A note on the kitchen counter explains you're at Aunt Regina's collecting Ben who had been there for a sleepover. I head to the bathroom and run the water. A hot, steamy soak will help soothe my puffy face, but I need something else to balance out my feelings.

Back in my room, I pick up my pills from the bedside table. If I take these now, they'll take at least 2 days to kick in and I don't think I can batten down all these emotions for the next 48 hours. Suddenly, I remember the little tin in my backpack. The edibles James gave me at Jessica's camp out party.

I reach for the tin hesitantly. I take a small bite off the corner. It's fruity smell certainly doesn't mask its overpowering taste. Chewing it as quickly as possible, I return to the bathroom. Adding some bubbles into the running water, I slowly undress. Stepping into the bath, I let the hot water soothe my aches. I lean my head back onto the cushioned pillow and stretch out my toes. Breathing calm in and letting stress out with every breath. I repeat the process wishing this coping technique to work, I'm running out of options.

Muffled voices announce you and Ben have returned. I don't know how long I've been in here, but it seems like hours. Omg, have I been here for hours? Stoned in the bath, unaware of time floating by? A light knock on the door interrupts my thought process. "Are you in there, Chelsie?" Your soft tone comforting, even through the door.

"Just in the bath Mom, I'll be out soon." I reassure you. Paranoia grabs hold of me and I sense the door handle move so slowly even though it's not actually moving. At least I don't think it is. Or is it? Looking around, I grab my towel from the toilet seat. Holding it in front of me, shielding my modesty from the imminent exposure of the door opening. I wait. Nothing. I peek above the towel and look in the door's direction. Nothing. The radio in the kitchen is playing soulful Adele.

"Take your time, honey. Ben's gonna help me set up dinner. I'm making chicken pot pie." Your footsteps fade away from the door. I allow my entire body to slip into the bath, muffling the sound of my giggles.

Chicken pot pie is my absolute favorite, and I realize I am starving. Pulling myself out of the bath, I grab the plush gray towel from the railing, surveying my face in the mirror. The hot steam has done its job. My skin has a rosy red glow as though I've enjoyed a facial and not spent the last few hours bawling my eyes out. My eyeballs however are another story. Small red blood vessels cut through the brilliant whites of my eyes. I rub them gently, but they hurt. My eyelids feel tight as though they've shrunken a little from all the crying. I get dressed, slowly. Mainly because I can't seem to get my coordination together. Another chuckle escapes me and I accept my gummy has indeed taken effect.

My clumsiness is now something new to mask throughout dinner. How fun. Oops, the giggling is back. I'm not sure if I'll be able to hide this. The irony is I'll never know if I fooled you or not, nevertheless here I come!

After rinsing out the bath and dumping the dirty laundry in my room, I join you with Ben in the kitchen.

"Oh Chelsie, you look so refreshed. The trip to your sister clearly did you the world of good. Even your eyes are sparkling." You kiss me on the forehead, holding your arms around my shoulders. Taking me in, assessing I'm still in one piece. Immediately, a new bout of paranoia surfaces. Have you realized I'm high? I try to act as normal as possible.

"Only 2 more days." Ben wraps his arms around my waist from behind and gives me an extra tight squeeze. He's excited.

I reach back with my right hand and ruffle his hair.

"Oh yes, your birthday! How old will you be this year Ben? Eleven? Are you Eleven already?" I tease him and laugh as he scrunches up his face and folds his arms across his chest.

"You know I'm not 11 Chelsie. Stop being silly. I'm going to be a teenager and you as well as Mom need to realize I'm mature now and will need to be treated accordingly." His tone is serious. This is not something to joke about.

"Ben, you know Chelsie is just teasing you. We both agree how mature you are. No one is questioning your maturity ok?" Your voice instantly soothes Ben's furrowed brow.

I laugh as he sticks his tongue out at me, heading back to the living room tv. "Has he been like this all week?" I sit down at the table and watch you stirring a little more cream into the saucepan. Your hair looks lighter. Strands of gold, forming loose curls around your face.

"Yeah, he is so excited about this party. Can you believe twenty-two people have rsvp'd? I didn't know Ben even had so many friends." Personally, I don't doubt that Ben is very popular at school with his easygoing nature, but it's more likely that kids are obsessed with the new laser tag center where you're hosting his party.

"Who wouldn't want to be friends with Ben? That's the real question." You nod your agreement. Your cheeks puff up and glow as your smile widens. Ben is your easy child. Apart from his allergies, you never need to worry about him. He's kind to others and gets on with everyone.

"What things do we still need to prepare for the party?" I'm not really interested, but I know by asking this, you will sort through the lists in your head and I will only be required to nod or hum my agreement. My giggles have subsided and a very lazy haze has now descended upon me.

No longer focused on your lists of party bags and sandwiches, an image of Luke crosses my mind and at once, little sensations of happiness dance through my veins. I glance back at you, serving up dinner. Still chattering eagerly about the party. Luckily for me, you're oblivious to the 'experience' I'm feeling right now. I concentrate as best I can throughout dinner, trying to comment on the conversation with you and Ben. Fortunately, you attribute my lack of to exhaustion and usher me off to bed as soon as I've finished eating.

Climbing into bed, I let go. I submit to the overwhelming feeling that everything is going to be alright. Stretching out my toes as if I can literally feel them extend. Rotating my neck, the stiffness that is constantly there stretches like magic. Using my three fingers, I pulse the tight skin on the back of my neck. Releasing the tension, I work my hands down under my chin all the way to my shoulders. Feeling more relaxed than I have in a long time.

I roll sideways, embracing myself. *It's ok Chelsie, you're going to be ok.* I reassure myself. I dream of myself floating further and further away until I'm nothing. Not even the smallest spec of dirt. Peace descends upon me, and I close my eyes, grateful for this moment.

Chapter 23

This morning I've woken feeling calm. The edible chased away my dark feelings, allowing me some respite to relax. I'm not over excited manic and not down in the dumps depressed, just calm. I can't remember experiencing this before and I lay in bed for the next hour, enjoying the peaceful sensation.

I hear your voice murmuring in the kitchen. I throw back the covers and wiggle my feet into my fuzzy slippers.

"I've got to go. I'll talk to you later." Your hushed tones echo down the hall. "Yes, ok, you too." You place your mobile on the counter as I walk into the open archway. Your cheeks are a soft rosy pink and a small, almost secret smile plays on your lips. Looking up from the counter, you catch me staring.

"Good morning, Chelsie. How are you today? Did you get a good night's sleep?" Your tone is light, but the barrage of questions indicates you would rather not explain who was on the phone. The rosy hue on your cheeks deepens and I realize you're blushing.

"I slept amazing, actually. Like the best I have in a long time." I open the cupboard and grab a tea cup.

"There's nothing quite like getting back to your own bed after traveling, that's for sure." I nod in agreement, but I'm pretty sure my sleep had more to do with James' little treat than the orthopedic mattress on my bed.

"What about you?" I ask. Your eyes quickly dart towards your mobile. "How did you sleep?" Your face relaxes and I almost giggle out loud at the panic in your eyes. You thought I was about to ask about the phone call! I know it's mean, but I am enjoying watching you squirm a little. That's what you get for keeping secrets!

"Is it time to go pick up my cake yet?" Only just out of bed, Ben is keen to get the party organizing started.

"It won't be ready 'til this afternoon, but you can help me make space in the fridge for it after breakfast. How does that sound?" You offer him.

He looks over at me and rolls his eyes. "It sounds like work. That's how it sounds." He sighs heavily. I give him a subtle wink as I place my index finger against my lips, encouraging him not to interrupt me.

"Actually, Mom, I was hoping to take Ben out today for a walk with me after breakfast. You don't mind, do you? I just wanna spend some time with him before he's all grown up tomorrow." I smile at you and know that you won't be able to resist my teasing and playful tone.

Opening the fridge, you survey the packed shelves.

"This needs a complete clean out anyway, so if you take Ben, then I'll clean this mess while you're gone. This afternoon, we can all go for lunch when we collect the cake. Is that a plan?" You look towards Ben for his approval.

"Sounds like a great plan to me." Ben winks at me, happy to have escaped the clear out session.

"Maybe we could invite Aunt Regina to join us. Is that who you were speaking to earlier?" Your eyes meet mine and I hold your gaze.

"Sure, I'll text her now and see if she's free." Sly move on your part to neither confirm nor deny if she had indeed been on the call from earlier. I fully intend to stare this out with you, but you pick up your phone and begin texting, eager to avoid any more questions. You place your phone back on the counter. "I must see if the laundry is dry before I forget." You announce awkwardly, heading towards the basement steps. "I'll see you both when you get back from your walk." Your voice trails further as you descend each step.

I almost burst out laughing but do my best to contain it, to avoid questions from Ben.

"Thanks Chels, what is Mom on? Am I right?" He encourages jovially. "Like as if I want to clean out the fridge. Get a grip, Mom." A large snort escapes me and the two of us burst out laughing. You're going to have your hands full over the next year or five. I think Ben is keen to grow up as fast as he can, with as much sass as he can get away with. I'm a little sad I won't get to watch these inevitable tug-o-wars between you two.

"I'm going to wash and get ready. I'll meet you out front in twenty minutes, ok?" I inform him. He nods his agreement whilst still shoveling cereal into his mouth. My heart tightens as I take the perfect photo of him in my mind. Right there in the kitchen, with his milky mustache, my heart feels like it might burst with love.

❧

"Where are we going?" Ben skips by my side excitedly.

"Hopefully you'll see real soon." I reassure him and indeed I hope he will. As we round the corner onto Luke's Street, I spot him jumping up in the corner of his yard as soon as he sees us approaching. His tail is wagging wildly. He runs back and forth along the chain link, eagerly waiting for us to reach our spot.

Under the big oak tree, I lay out the gingham picnic blanket I had packed into my back pack earlier. I sit down and pat the space beside me, inviting Ben to join. Hesitantly, he sits next to me. Luke is poking his paws through the chain link whilst simultaneously licking my fingers that I've poked through to greet him.

"Why are we here?" Ben looks at me. I notice the downward pull of his lips into a slight frown. I think he was hoping for something more exciting than this.

Dear Mom, I'm sorry

Smoothing the blanket in front of me, I explain. "I want you to meet my friend Luke." I can feel my eyes water slightly, but my voice sounds strong, even.

"When I was away at Hannah's I was worried about him and I realized I needed someone to look after him when I might not be here." I explained.

"But how do you know him? Does his owner not take care of him? How did you become friends? What will I need to do?" Ben's inquisitive mind imagines all scenarios. I do my best to answer his questions as honestly as possible.

"I met him before school ended and I've been visiting him ever since. I've only heard his owner call for him from inside. To be honest, he sounds a bit like a grump. Before I left for Hannah's, I cleaned his paws and tried to trim his nails. They looked like they hadn't been done for a long time, so I'm not sure they're taking very good care of him." Ben slips his fingers through the metal squares and gently pets Luke's fluffy neck.

Luke pulls back, ducking his head and greedily licks Ben's fingers. Ben laughs loudly.

"He likes me!" He sits up on his knees, eager to get closer to Luke.

"I knew you'd be great friends." I take out a few snacks from my backpack and place them on our blanket. Ben and I take turns tempting Luke with our treats. Teddy bear grahams appear to be the tastiest, but I'm sure the apple slices are healthier for his diet.

"Can I visit him anytime? Or only when you're away at Hannah's or Dad's? Do I need to keep him a secret from mom?" A feeling of love surges through me. Now that he has established his bond with Luke, he wants to know the boundaries to protect it.

I love how clear and focused Ben's mind is. It's my favorite thing about him. Could you tell him that later? Please tell him how much I admired his logical reasoning and willingness to share emotions.

I know as his big sister he thinks he learned so much from me, but the truth is, Ben has taught me about being in wonder and in awe at the beauty of the world. I truly treasure how he savors moments, as if to make them last just a few seconds longer. We all need a bit more of that in our lives.

"Now that you are friends, you can visit him whenever you want but try to stay discreet ok? I always sit here, slightly camouflaged by this tree, so no one in the neighborhood notices me. I'm worried if Luke's owner saw me, he might not let me hang out anymore. Or if mom found out, she'd worry Luke might bite me, or give me fleas or a million other made up worries that only moms can dream up." I smile at him. I want him to understand I'm teasing, but also to keep this special secret so we don't lose it. He nods solemnly, taking in my words.

He leans his head against the fence.

"We'll keep our new friendship on the down-low. What do you think, Luke?" Luke's long pink tongue licks the side of Ben's cheek, pushing through the metal and Ben laughs quietly.

I'm relieved. I've found Luke someone to look out for him and I've left Ben my best friend. Standing up, I wipe my pants down from our snack crumbs. Mission complete, I'm ready to head home.

Ben helps me to fold the blanket and we reassure Luke we will be back soon. Maybe not tomorrow because of Ben's birthday party, but definitely the day after, Ben promises. Luke tilts his head to one side as though understanding every word.

Ben talks eagerly of his party on the walk home and I am grateful to still be here. To watch him celebrate one more year.

∂∘∞

Climbing into bed, I realize I'm still calm. I'm not sure if it's the side effects from yesterday's gummy or if in some way my mind has found peace. Come to terms with my decision, the inevitable. Whichever it is, it feels good.

I'm able to reflect on the last few days and just like a crazy game of Tetris, all the pieces are finally falling into place.

Even sharing my secret with Ben today felt like a parting gift. Once you let a secret out, you can never put it back again. You can't take the new information back from someone's mind and make them forget it. Luke is no longer just my concern or worry. Now I've shared that with Ben, he shares my responsibility too.

I realize this might be how you feel about whoever you were talking to this morning. That person right now is just yours. As soon as you share that information with

Dear Mom, I'm sorry

Hannah, Ben, and me, we'll all have questions and opinions, just like Ben did with me today. It will force you to question your own intentions and actions. I accept that you're not ready for that yet. Not that you're lying, but maybe you're just enjoying the simplicity of your secret, just as I had been with Luke.

Chapter 24

All day, I watched you running around making sure everything was perfect for Ben and his friends. You even had labels printed for each participant, with their name and team color. There were 4 groups altogether. They all had so much fun. You had prepared snacks and games for after the laser tag battle. By the time the kids went home, each and every one of them was ready for bed and their parents were so thankful.

When you've hosted mine and Hannah's parties, I've always attended as a participant. Watching everyone else, constantly studying, learning. I don't know that I've ever watched you like I did this afternoon.

Today I saw you through those other parents' eyes. How it appeared you had everything under control. Pretty (yes, you are Mom, just accept it!), organized and calm. Effortlessly running games, giving out prizes, juice boxes and hugs. Whatever someone needed, you were there.

I knew it was your nerves and your anxiety fueling you. You run on nervous energy. Your worry for me is not exceptional. You worry for all of us. You love and you love big. You have the same concern, worry and care towards Ben and Hannah. It's how you show us your love.

Watching through some of the other mom's eyes, I saw a strong, courageous woman and I now realize that I'm not observant as I thought.

I'm not smart at all because I missed the most noticeable thing about you. You are a warrior mom. You fight for each one of us. Your worry that anything could happen, means you live to be prepared. To protect and to defend us if necessary. In all my years of watching and studying people, I've never noticed it before.

The fiercest love.

You love us more than yourself. I can't even imagine an emotion on that scale. That big. It must be electrifying. A smile spreads across my face at the mere idea of it.

Unconditional love, no matter what we could say or do, you love us.

You've spent your whole life pushing your boundaries and capabilities, yet you give us your pride so easily. I wish you could give yourself that love. The one you give us. I don't know why everyone around you is deserving of it. I see someone who has earned it, time and time again. Be proud of who you are. Stop accepting blame for everything that happened before. Give yourself grace.

I know you are hurt reading this now. No doubt, my words are blurred with your tears, but this is my parting gift to you. Forgiveness. Forgive yourself, ok? Yes your genes are my genes, but you are never to blame for how I couldn't cope. How I couldn't be normal. You didn't *make me* like this. It's not your fault.

Tomorrow I'm going to treat you to a spa day. Facials, pedicures and a massage at Elegant Touch. The exclusive salon is not your usual nail bar, and I am excited to bring you. I wish I could say these words to you tomorrow. Encourage you to accept the vision of how others see you. As a warrior. Strong enough to support 3 children, thrive in your career, be a great friend, a sister, an aunt.

Someone that people are genuinely glad they've run into. Like when you're in the supermarket. It takes us 20 minutes to shop but 2 hours to chat with everyone you meet. You don't want to be deemed negative or rude. You always have a kind, encouraging word for others. Your love is big and in return people love you. Everyone except who matters most. Yourself.

Tomorrow, when our day out is finished, you'll hug me and thank me. I am going to hug you and say, I love you mom, but what I really want to say is forgive yourself. We all do.

Chapter 25

Aunt Regina is coming over for lunch. Yesterday at Ben's party she invited him for another sleepover with Jaxon. Ben's eyes lit up at the idea of all you can eat ice cream buffets and dance parties that are a favorite for us all when we visit with her.

I had secretly texted her earlier in the week so we could be alone for our appointments this afternoon at the salon. I also could not complete my last act if Ben was in the house.

I wanted our last day together to be just me and you. A day for you to feel appreciated as a mom. So that when you wake tomorrow to a real-life nightmare, some piece of you will try to fathom that this has nothing to do with my love for you. Or your worth as a mom. It is not a by-product of anyone's past mistakes. It's not karma, Mom. It's not you. It's definitely all me. I'm going to let myself go. Stop the deceit, stop the acting. Please make sure you do the same. Let it go.

❧❧

"We're here." Aunt Regina's voice hollers from down the hallway. I close my notebook and skip to the stairs landing.

"Hey Jaxon." Are you excited to have a sleepover with Ben? He lays his head against his shoulder with a slight shrug. A little shy.

"I think he's in the living room." Descending the stairs, I hold my hand out to him. "Shall we go see if we can find him?" I take his hand and we toddle towards the living area. Jaxon is the cutest baby I've ever seen. I know you say he's not a baby anymore, but with that cherub face, He's always going to be a baby to me.

"Ben, look who's here!" Jaxon climbs up onto the couch beside Ben and links his arm with Ben.

Ben turns the tv over to the cartoon channel. "Dis one." Jaxon calls excitedly as police puppies fly across the screen.

I leave them chatting happily on the couch and come find you and Aunt Regina in the kitchen. I overhear her as I approach.

"So, when are you seeing him again?" The creak in the hallway announces my presence.

You glance in my direction and back at Regina.

"In my dreams." You laugh heartily.

Your reaction is flawless. Good acting! Can't say the same for aunt Regina though. Her cheeks are on fire and her lower left lash is visibly shaking. I join in your laughter but more at aunt Regina's face than anything else.

"Who were you dreaming about? Tell me!" I demand in a teasing voice. You catch aunt Regina's eye and with a slight rise to your eyebrow, you give her a confident nod.

"Kevin Costner. Aunt Regina was thinking we should watch Robin Hood, prince of thieves tonight after our spa date. Coincidentally, I was dreaming about him last night. Maybe we should watch it?" You suggest, giggling at Aunt Regina.

You serve pasta from the pot onto our plates and we carry them to the table. Aunt Regina pours you both a glass of wine and a small tasting glass for me. I'm not a fan of alcohol. It reminds me of Jessica's party last year. The could have-been's. The dashed hopes and dreams.

The last day or two I might have had a few more nibbles of the edibles James gifted me. They induce a little bit of paranoia so I only take small bites.

I keep expecting to be caught out. For my plan to be exposed. My eye twitches. Immediately I look at you and back to aunt Regina to see if you either of you noticed. Of course, no one else is watching people that intensely. Like I do. Everyone else takes words or actions at face value. They're not looking for hidden meanings or twitching eyes.

I raise my mini glass. "To you, Mom, for everything you do for us. Cheers." Aunt Regina clicks her glass with mine and slowly you raise yours too.

"Cheers." We all chime together.

"Thank you Chelsie. I love you all so much." The sun shining on your face catches the blond highlights glistening in your hair. You're happy, you're hopeful, you're ready.

I eat hungrily, definitely a side effect from my earlier nibbles. The pasta is so good. Long tendrils of fettucine smothered in a creamy sauce, with mushrooms, peppers and mini tomatoes. A real taste of the Mediterranean. The oven timer chimes as I spoon the last mouthful from my bowl.

"That'll be Ben and Jaxon's mac and cheese." Pushing back your chair, you put on your silicone glove and remove the glass pan from the oven.

"Ben, lunchtime," you call, placing the tray on the granite countertop.

I watch in a slight haze as you make a fuss over Jaxon, tickling and kissing him. The boys sit at the breakfast bar, eating mac and cheese whilst making silly faces at each other. You and Aunt Regina chat as you clean things away and she helps Jaxon make less mess!

"Have a great time at Aunt Regina's Ben." I wrap my arms around him from behind and kiss him on his cheek. He pretends to pull away from my affection, but I know this will be our last goodbye. "I'll miss you ok? I love you squillions." I clear my throat, faking a small cough, clearing a tickle.

"Jeesh, I'm only going for one night Chels. I'll be back tomorrow." He playfully swats me away while simultaneously rolling his eyes at Jaxon, who laughs in delight. I bend down and kiss his cute, pudgy cheeks.

"See you later, alligator." I offer my raised hand and Jaxon responds with a strong high five. "Good job Jax." I ruffle his hair before turning towards aunt Regina. "Thanks Gigi for taking Ben so I can treat mom today." She embraces me. Rubbing her hand under my left shoulder blade, just like she used to when I was younger. When she would read me stories nestled in her lap.

"I love you." I whisper and squeeze her extra tight. Inhaling the heady scent of her perfume, brings tears to my eyes. A smell I shall forever associate with safety, love and kindness.

"I love you more than sunshine." She answers. I nod as she plants a kiss on my forehead.

Walking toward the stairs, I pause momentarily, looking back. It's just a boring lunchtime scene in our kitchen, but I snap a bittersweet picture in my memory to treasure for always.

꩜

In my room, feelings flood me. Washing over me like drops of rain falling from my eyes. The end of my nerves feel raw and exposed. I'm jittery and shaking. I sit on the edge of my bed, one leg folded under me and the other firm on the floor. I try to relax. To stop the trembling coursing through my veins. Images haunt my vision. Aunt Regina's trusting face. Ben happily pushing me away.

You're so selfish. My guilt taunts me.

You'll ruin their lives. My empathy chimes in. But what about me? I cry into my duvet.

See, like I said, you're selfish. My judgement replies. I deserve more too. My ego defends me.

You're never happy. You hated not having feelings and now you're having too many. My brain accuses me.

This is it. Here it is. The spiral out of control. I knew it was coming. I just didn't know when. I hear the music of impending doom playing in my mind. The darkness is returning. Mean, destructive and unsafe behavior is on its way. Shame, humiliation and hate will soon follow. And to top it all off, regret, embarrassment and disappointment will pile on top of me until I can no longer get out of bed.

The emergency services will be called, and a transfer to the hospital will be arranged. A little vacation for me and I'll be feeling better in no time.

Everyone reassuring you that this time, they'll get the medications right. Reminding you how well I've been coping these last few years. All the platitudes and lies will return. I can't bear to imagine myself stepping back into my role. My fake life. Determination fuels me to clean myself up and to get ready for our afternoon out. Our last Mother-daughter day.

Chapter 26

The spa experience is amazing. I really love the citrus jelly foot bath. In general, I don't like to be touched, so I took an extra nibble of James contraband and I must confess the massage experience felt other-worldly. It's also diluted my feelings from earlier. I don't feel as exhausted as I did before. A little more level-headed and balanced is where I'm at now. Which is great because I really want to enjoy this experience with you.

"Whatcha smiling at?" You ask me.

Opening my eyes, I meet your gaze. "Just feeling happy." I blurt, without thinking.

The largest grin stretches across your face. My eyes fill with tears at your reaction. You pat my hand, reassuring me there's no need to be embarrassed by my happy tears.

You misunderstood. They are tears of sorrow. For I realize that in sharing my happiness, I've given you hope. Hope where there is none.

Tomorrow is going to hit you even harder, if that's possible. I should have been more careful in my preparing you. I didn't mean to give you false hope.

On our way home, we order soup and sandwich combos from Panera. A treat for a late evening snack.

"I still feel stuffed from lunch. Would you mind if I went for my walk?" I ask as you unlock the front door. Before, it gets too dark for me to say goodbye to Luke.

"Not at all. Shall I come with you?" You offer.

I shake my head and wave my hands. "No need for us to both suffer. You get in your jammies and I'll see you on the couch for Robin Hood in twenty minutes. How about that?" I negotiate. Eager to deter any further delays or offers to accompany me.

"If you're sure?" You shrug. You're at ease. Relaxed. You think I'm happy.

As soon as I change my shoes, I'm back outside. Running all the way to Luke's. Holding in my tears, I arrive at the big tree. My sadness deepens. Luke isn't out. I dig my fingernails hard into my arms.

Don't cry. You're fine. I'm so angry with myself. Weeks of planning have gone into this and I'm messing it up on the last day! Instead of showing you how despairing my situation is, I have somehow thrown hope into the mix. I should have come and visited Luke yesterday or earlier before we went out. Now I won't even have the chance to say goodbye.

Leaning my head against the tree, I close my eyes and think of the times we shared. I'm glad Ben will visit. Luke will know I sent him. He might not understand where I went, but he's smart. He'll remember I brought Ben and introduced them. Somehow he will sense it. He'll understand I didn't just forget him.

A loud yelp echoes from within the house and the front door opens. Luke! He must have been scratching at the door, asking his owner to come out. Maybe he intuitively felt me here? His owner slams the door behind him.

Luke runs towards me, and I release my pent-up tears. All the hurt and sadness I've been suppressing flows unashamedly. I hang on to the fence with both of my hands.

Pushing my face into the metal chain link, Luke licks my tears, encouraging them to fall faster.

"This is it, Lukey Loo," I sob. Telling him how much he means to me and how I know he and Ben will bring comfort to each other. I thank him for allowing me to experience real friendship.

"I'll never forget you no matter where I am." I promise. I rub the back of my hand under my eye socket. It stings. The skin across it is tight. The tissue underneath it, inflamed and bruised.

Exhausted and wrecked I say goodbye.

"I love you, Luke. Look after Ben for me." I turn away and walk home not even attempting to hide the tears streaming down my face. The sound of Luke howling follows me home.

I sneak into the house quietly. Hoping to make it to the bathroom before you notice I'm home.

At the sink, I wash my ravaged face and apply a honey oatmeal mask to my raw skin. I change into pajama shorts and my Montana sweater, once back in my room.

Taking an extra-large nibble from my dwindling gummy supply. I chug down the glass of water on my bedside table. I'm hoping it will calm my inner grief. Or maybe some feelings can't be suppressed. Paused perhaps, but not stopped.

Like, have you ever noticed how easily people give their happy away but rarely their sadness or disappointment? If I was letting people steal my feelings, I'd only let them have the negative ones. I wouldn't care what they thought or felt because I would be too busy enjoying all my own feelings. There would be no time to worry about what others thought or might think or might do. No thanks. If I had feelings, then those are the only ones I would care about: my own! Maybe people would call me selfish.

"Ooooh, look over there." They would remark snarkily.

"Selfish Chelsie. Only ever pleases herself. Always, living her best life." People would look at me enviously. A giggle escapes me at the mere idea of anyone being jealous of me.

Wow, these edibles really do the job. My mouth is so dry. With my empty glass in hand, I head to the kitchen to refill it.

"Look at you go." Pride shines from your features.

Dear Mom, I'm sorry

"An evening walk, a facemask and even staying hydrated. Good for you, practicing that self-care!"

I roll my eyes at you, discouraging your praise. I'm in no mood to listen to how great you think I am right now.

"Ready for Robin Hood?" I am keen to distract from any further conversation. With every word and action, I feel as though I'm saying the wrong thing. You nod your head towards the small wicker basket on the table. You've filled it with my favorite flavored Pop Shoppe bottles and bags of candy. I pick it up, leading us into the living room.

The movie is perfectly apt. Even if we are watching it because I caught you in a lie. My edible has kicked in. I feel very caught up in this romantic fairy tale.

Imagine if we lived in a world where things were just and fair? When things go wrong, we do what needs to be done to put things right. Wouldn't that be something? Stealing and lying are sins, but when done for the right reasons, they are forgivable.

Sometimes we need to do the wrong thing for the right reasons.

The slow hum of your breathing is steady. Between Ben's birthday and my return from Hannah's, it has been an exhausting few days for you. I unfold the cream, soft lambswool blanket hanging on the back of the loveseat and drape it around you. Pulling the cover closer, you smile sleepily. "Did I miss the movie?" Your voice is barely a whisper.

"Shhhh." I kiss you on the cheek. "Relax here. Go back to sleep, Mom. I love you."

"You too Chels. I love you so much." You reply, still half asleep.

I turn the tv off but leave the lamp on. It's soft glow lights your face perfectly. I snap one last memory to take with me on my next journey. I'm not certain if there's a *God* or not, but at the same time; I think there's something out there. Something more than this. A place where I make sense. Just because I don't fit in this world doesn't mean I won't fit in somewhere else.

Back in my room, I stare at my glassy eyes in the reflection from the mirror. I'm not going to lie, but I think this gummy may have made me a little euphoric. I can see why people say you need to be so careful with dosing the right amount. I'm going to assume I have definitely taken more than the required *relaxing* amount.

Closing my eyes, I envision my next life as a butterfly. Flying through the air, in a whirl of color. A symbol of change and hope to those around me. I like this idea. It's my very own fairy tale.

Right now, I'm a weak caterpillar. Siting vulnerable, hiding from any prey. But soon, very soon. I will enter a chrysalis of my own. A new journey will begin. That's the way I want you to think of me. Like the strong Monarch, spreading my wings, fluttering beautifully around you.

I remove three envelopes from my drawer and bring them into my closet. One marked for Dad, one for Hannah, and lastly, one for Ben. I place each one of them on the boxes that I've sorted through.

There's no letter for you, so don't search for it. This notebook, its contents, my truth, is hopefully more than any letter could ever have given you.

I will leave it to your discretion how much of this you will share with others. I've told them what I need them to know. That I love them. How I wish I could have been different. Telling them how sorry I am that I am not strong enough to stay and watch them.

I must follow my own journey now. They'll have so many questions for you and I hope I have left you with enough insight to share with them.

Or you could choose to lie. Maybe you don't want them to see me as the weak little caterpillar. Or to wonder if my entire life with them was an act. I don't know how that would make Ben feel. What I am certain of is that you will find the right words. The right angle or perspective to help him cope and understand.

I know you'll be grieving, but they're still going to need their mom. Just like you will need them more than ever. And aunt Regina. And Mr. whatever his name is that makes you blush. But you'll still see me. In the yard, amongst your summer flowers, spreading my wings, soaring. I'll visit often so you won't ever need to miss me.

Dear Mom, I'm sorry

Chapter 27

This is it. My last entry. In a few hours, a knock on the door will awaken you from your sleep on the couch. When you open the door, the paramedic will talk to you in hushed tones while his partner runs upstairs to my bedroom. It sounds incredulous, but I actually found a willing helper on one of the mental health forums. Some of the more prepared groups have an option to ask a fellow member for help.

Someone might want an envelope mailed after their passing. Or a message written posthumously on their social media.

In my case, I wanted to ensure you wouldn't have to be the one to find me. It was easy to arrange for Ben to be out of the house, but I still had to ensure somebody else found me before you did. That's where the helper comes in. They will make the crisis call.

A crisis call is when a person calls 911 and informs them that they think an individual might have hurt themselves. You can request your helper to give specific instructions, such as directions to your room. Medications taken, etc. For me, I needed someone to time that call.

It's 11:30 pm now and I want the ambulance team to be called at 5. Early enough so that you won't have woken yet, but late enough to allow my mix of pills to do their work.

I retrieve my pill stash from the bag taped underneath my vanity. Carefully opening the little Ziploc and pouring the pills into my glass ring holder. I don't know which are which, but over the last 6 months I have snuck and squirreled away enough of them. Sleeping pills, pain pills, and even a few of your anti-anxiety meds that I took here and there. Not enough of one type to draw attention but all together I have an impressive collection.

Quietly, I slip out of my room to the kitchen. I grab a glass from the cupboard and the bottle of vodka from the top shelf in the pantry.

Returning to my room, I pause in the living room entryway.

"Goodbye Mom, I love you." I whisper hoarsely to your angelic face, sleeping on the couch. Your last peaceful sleep for some time.

Tears run down my face as I pour the vodka into my glass. I have everything I need. Logging into the crisis call support page, I prepare for my final curtain call.

Clicking on the envelope icon, I choose the send new message option. My helper is Georgina. She's not online, but it's still early and she knows tonight is the night. I include our address in the message along with the time to make the call. I hit send and log off. Tonight, I have zero interest in reading any of the message boards. My final act is complete, I prepare my cocktail.

I can't remember which pills are which, but I'm pretty sure the pink and blue ones are the sleeping pills. Opening them, allowing their powder to fall into my glass. I open one more and then another until there are no red and blue cased pills left in my possession. I swoosh the powder into the vodka with my fingers and take a gulp.

Fire burns my throat as I force myself to swallow the potent mixture. My gag reflex kicks in and I close my mouth tightly, unrelenting. I take smaller sips. I've got time. With the alcohol coursing through my veins, I feel energized.

I swallow one oblong and one round pill to help get the party started. I line up the next few and check my watch. 11:50pm. I'll take another 3 at midnight, then 4 at 12:15 and so on until sleep beckons me.

It seems foolish now, but I spent so much time planning today. The ideal day and time for this type of event to take place.

The weekend is when the outside world slows down the most. Have you ever noticed that? Tonight allows you a couple of days to come to terms with things before needing to make those uncomfortable calls, to your work, to my school. Hannah will be able to travel immediately. Aunt Regina will be free to help you and Ben. That's the upside of passing your life as an observer. Sometimes I see what others can't and if I could sense pride, this is what I would be most proud of. My ability to see what people need.

Speaking of pride, I am going to ask you one last favor and I feel like I have you over a barrel here. I think you'll have to agree. Please promise to always remember me with pride. Even these last actions of mine. Despite my inability to be like others, I know what's right; I know what's wrong. I tried and tried again, so finally I have earned the right to end the game. To have the courage to speak up for myself and live the way I choose, or not.

I knew when the time was right, I could leave in peace because you brought me up to learn from my environment and I did that better than anyone I know. I've prepared and explained to you as best as I can. I hope amongst these words you'll find the answer to any residual questions you may have. And most of all, I'm proud that I am brave enough to stop this vicious cycle, that otherwise would never end.

On the front of this notebook, I've been scribbling since I stopped taking my medication. I am going to scribble on it now whilst I finish my drink and take my next set of pills. I hope the entire cover fills with scribbles, so that I let go of all my hurt and pain. If it's filled, you'll know, I went in peace.

I will always be proud to be your daughter and I hope that's how you'll remember me. With pride.

I love you more than all the words in this journal could ever express. I hope somewhere amongst them, I've proved to you that I made the right choice.

I love you Mom,

I'm sorry.

Chelsie x o x

P.S. So many scribbles and I can barely move now. I'm so sleepy. I imagine my scribbles like threads of silk. Weaving a nest, a cocoon around me. G'night Mom.

෮ The end ෯

Follow Mary O'Hora on Goodreads for info
on upcoming releases and sneak peeks!

Please Chelsie,

Forgive me.

COMING SOON

Dear Mom, I'm sorry

If you or someone you know is in crisis or at risk of suicide, please reach out.

The *Suicide & Crisis Lifeline* – call or text them at **988.** (USA)
Crisistextline.org - *Text **HOME** to 741741 from anywhere in the United States, anytime. Crisis Text Line is here for any crisis. A live, trained Crisis Counselor receives the text and responds, all from our secure online platform. The volunteer Crisis Counselor will help you move from a hot moment to a cool moment.* (USA)

The Canadian Association for Suicide Prevention (CASP) *Call 1-833-456-4566 provides advocacy, communication and education for suicide prevention and life promotion through educational materials and resources.* **(Canada)**

lifeline.org.au – *Call 13 11 14 or text 0477 13 11 14 for confidential one-to-one text or chat with a trained Lifeline Crisis Supporter.* **(Australia)**

crisistextline.uk - *Text **SHOUT** to 85258 in the UK to text with a trained Crisis Volunteer.* **(United Kingdom)**

Call *your health care professional and make an appointment for long-term support.*

Talk *with friends and family, let people around you know how they can help.*

Communicate. *Keep the conversation going no matter how difficult it is. Only by communicating and educating each other will we remove the stigma from mental health challenges.*

What inspired this book?

It's tough to communicate. We might say the wrong thing. Our words have consequences. But so does our silence. As a mom myself, I encouraged my children to be well behaved, use their manners, and follow the rules.

One day on a road trip my eldest asked. "Ok we know the rules, but who's making them? Maybe we're all in a simulation!" I looked at her face and she was serious, partly anyway. It was surprising to me that she thought so differently. To wonder and question everything. My generation just did as we were told. Followed the line and sucked things up. It kind of irked me that she was basically questioning it all. I have always believed in free speech so even though I didn't agree with all of her ways to look at things, she got me thinking, And I continued thinking and wondering.

As she grew, she encouraged me to look at things from her perspective and I realized that despite the rules, the disciplining, the lessons I had tried to teach her, she had become her own person. She held some different views from me. She challenged me when she felt someone should. She was no longer my mini-me.

I had 3 younger children as well. We managed to muddle through times as best as any family with 4 kids and 2 dogs can. My elder child would continue to discuss different views, trying to expand my more ridged opinions.

As discussions of mental health became more commonplace, she would attempt to broach subjects and conversations with me. She was always questioning me, why this, or who decided that. I remember when she was younger my husband remarking that she answered back a lot, and I said, "She's not talking back, she's asking for an explanation and that's allowed. If we don't teach our children to ask questions when they don't understand something, then they'll be easily led by every person they meet."

I myself struggled with some childhood trauma and had been in and out of counseling or therapy since I was 11 years old. I would feel well and be a warrior, and then my PTSD would kick in and I would be a mess. All of this was camouflaged by my boundless energy and manic, obsessive behavior. I found amazing ways to 'cope', to improve and do better. I was adamant my kids would never need to struggle like I did.

But they did. Like every single one of us on this earth. They also had periods that were overwhelming, difficult to navigate. How could I keep them safe?

My eldest and her talk of mental health felt insulting. Kids always making excuses for themselves. I gave her every support, every encouragement, and now some diagnosis could excuse her lazy, uninterested, hormonal behavior? The world today. Clearly, I had failed as a mom. A job I thought I was so good at!

Very luckily for me, I brought up a fierce young lady who is not afraid to speak her mind when it matters most and she challenged me until little by little, my narrow mind opened. But as it opened a whole new set of concerns set in.

If the rules and outdated social skills no longer apply, how will I parent my other children? I had constantly told my eldest, you should do this or you should do that and I had been very wrong. What in the world do I tell them now?

I realized that my eldest had taught me some of my best life lessons simply by asking me questions. She didn't ask them to be annoying or rude, but to better understand things in her mind. At that moment, I knew the old rules no longer applied.

I needed to stop telling my children what they should do, how they should feel, and I needed to start asking them questions. Find out WHO they wanted to be.

Not only did my relationship with my children improve, but I myself started to ask questions. More and more questions eventually led me to seek more modern therapies and medicines for my own struggles. My life changed. Thankfully, I no longer recognize the Mom I used to be but I never forget her cause she taught me so much and she tried so hard.

I'm much prouder of the mom I am today. What mattered more; How 'good' my parenting was or how happy my children were? Imagine If I never listened, and I just kept telling?

Now I try to parent with my 'Ask don't tell' method. Where I ask questions instead of only giving my opinion. I mean I'm still going to have a say but it's going to be a conversation now and not a lecture (my kids may disagree with me here)!

What if? What if I had not raised such a strong young woman? What if I never adapted or evolved by listening to her, by searching for answers to her questions together?

Dear Mom, I'm sorry

Every day, I am thankful that my beautiful, precious daughter was courageous enough to keep asking me questions until finally I listened. I've been listening ever since!

I was so focused on what I needed to do to protect them that I didn't even take their needs or desires into account. Not because I didn't love them, but because, like the mom in the story, I love big. My love can suffocate if I don't take a breath. I too am learning, just like they are. We're all learning and sharing together. We still have differences and like all families we still have bad days, but we keep the conversation going every day.

Every single day we communicate, we continue to learn, and we talk about mental health. There are no taboo or off limit thoughts, feelings or subjects. There's no RIGHT or WRONG way to be. We're searching for answers together.

I've become an advocate for mental health and I strongly believe that supporting and encouraging one another will always be the right choice. With this story, I hope you will keep the conversation about mental health going. The healing, feeling well can bring us. The persistence to try alternative therapies or medicines. The grace to offer others, instead of judgement. Keep asking questions until those around us listen.

I am grateful every day that despite my own weaknesses; I raised children confident enough to question me and I promise to always be listening. Katie, Nicholas, Faith and Christian, thank you for teaching me how to be your mom x.

Mary O'Hora

Communicate

We don't have it figured out, but together we can. Next time you want to share your view or stance try it differently. Here are a few general questions to give you a helping hand in making your own.

- I would never want you to feel uncomfortable. Can you share with me some ways I could avoid doing that? It's important for me to support you.

- It's challenging for me when we have different views on a subject we both feel so strongly about. However, my relationship with you is more important than any of that. If I give you a 1 minute summary from my point, could you do the same for me? We don't need to discuss or argue about it after I just want to have a few days to think about things from your perspective, so I have a broader view.

- I struggle if you tell me lies. It really affects how much I can trust you. What could we do instead? What ideas do you have?

- When you slammed the door, I felt you were angry. Are you feeling ok right now? Is there something I can do to help you?

- I don't fully understand your interest in this. What is it that you enjoy?

- It's so disappointing that wasn't the solution. Shall we try to figure out the next step together?